Cheap Fish

Nanci E. LaGarenne

For James

Acknowledgments

This book would not have been possible without Donny D'Albora and the lowdown on all things fishing commercially. Thanks for the stories, your passionate honesty and for allowing me to combine a respected and endangered way of life with imagination.

Thanks to my "brother," Tommy, for your story of a whore boat.

To my grandmothers for encouraging my imagination. One told me she lived in a palace in Bari and the other told stories out of tealeaves in a Vermont kitchen.

Thanks, Mom, for making magic of ordinary days, sugar on snow and saving every poem I ever wrote. Dad, for proving tough guys still need love and songs and stories were dreams you wrote because you really did believe.

To my amazing sons, my greatest work ever. Jason, for believing in the impossible. Eric, for your gentle wisdom. Tina and Jen, my daughters- in- love, I am in awe of your brilliance.

To my granddaughter, Hailey Sage, who has taught me in her two and a half years that laughter is the best medicine, crayons are for peeling, love is all you need and redheads rock. Gram loves you.

To my sisters, Lin and Joie, for reading my books.

To Barbara Jean for telling me I could do it.

To James for remembering what matters.

Prologue

I hate people. That's why I fish. Well, fished. Before they regulated us to kingdom come and tore the heart and soul out of the commercial fishing industry. Industry is grandiose talk. We put food on the table. Commercial fishing is wearing; takes its toll on the body. You get beat up long lining, hauling lobster pots, dragging. The weather alone can pound the joy right out of you. We're like the US postal service, rain or shine, we go out. The trips are long and sometimes fruitless. Fishing is a gamble. There is no insurance plan, pension or retirement package. There is one big benefit. Pride in fishing and nobody can take that away from you.

I had some stellar years offshore. The peace you find on the open sea is priceless. No boss in a Brooks Brothers riding you, demanding every drop of blood. No backstabbers stepping over you to get ahead. On a boat, everyone is equal. There are no stars. The captain fishes right next to you. It's a joint effort. The more fish caught the more money in everyone's pocket when you pack out.

Fishing is romanticized. The whole sailor and mermaid myth. People like a good fish tale. Right below the surface is the dark side that every commercial fisherman knows. Friends that never made it home. Boats and crews lost to the unforgiving black fathoms. Families left behind without a livelihood or that all important buzzword, closure. It doesn't come, trust me. That wound remains open for a lifetime. The fragile hope that maybe their loved one is shipwrecked on a distant shore and will someday return? That's a movie.

We go back day after day and fish, no matter what. That's what we know. There is no choice after awhile. Even when we step away from fishing, it doesn't last. It's deep in the blood. You have to be out there on the sea. Assume you're coming back, with fish. Like I said, it's a gamble.

Fishermen have a bad reputation. Drunken sailor. Pirates and rum. Fishermen and bars go hand in hand. I pickled myself with the best of them. Between the drinking and the bum arm from dragging, I had to call it quits. Sooner than I planned, but then where fishing is concerned you don't get a definitive plan. You fish till your body tells you: "You're done Salty." That realization is hard to swallow. Suddenly you aren't getting any younger and you were born to fish. I wasn't about to take up golfing. I'm a hunter. I like extremes. Plus I have a bad temper. With my luck, some yuppie would crowd me on the ninth hole and I'd end up wrapping a club around his neck. No, I had to find a new endeavor that would keep my attention and not stagnate the old raison d'être.

I ate my slice of humble pie but I won't say I enjoyed it. Easy, I'm not, and I'm the first to admit it. Well, maybe the second. My ex liked to say, "Yeah, you're a day at the beach...Omaha Beach." So I like a fight. Bred in me. In the gene pool. Speaking of which, my old man had some sage advice. "Get out while you can, kid. The damp in your bones will cripple you. Start thinking about another way to earn a living."
Brilliant. Why didn't I think of that? Exactly what

else am I supposed to do? Fishing is all I know. The old man groomed me for it.

I held a fishing pole as soon as I could stand. I watched my father and older brother haul in their catch, such satisfaction on their faces. I wanted that feeling. And I would be lying if I said the money wasn't seductive. For a brief moment in time, I fought the bug. Fishing couldn't lure me in, pardon the pun. I was in charge of my destiny.

I explored another realm. The sky. Maybe I would become a pilot. Freedom in that, too. I am a natural born free spirit. But the pull of the sea was like a magnet. Something in me needed it. Called me like a relentless siren. Maybe it was predestined. What other path is there when your old man names you Dragger? I gave in. I fished. I am a commercial fisherman. A Salty. Well I was, until that night in Liars and the best proposition of my life came up. Now they call me something else. Captain Dragger Delray at your service. Partner aboard the finest whore boat off Montauk.

Chapter One

"On a scale of one to ten, how's the pain today, Dragger?"

"Bout a six. 'Fuck you' is always about a six."

The physical therapist smiled, as she rubbed a healthy blob of massage cream into her favorite client's unique tattoo. He moaned in ecstasy. "You got the spot," he said in a gravelly voice. "That's fucking magic. Excuse my French."

Chase smiled. "Oh was that French?" She kneaded his muscular bicep hard. "Sounds more like fishing talk if you ask me."

"Smart girl. Yeah, once upon a time it was magic out there…" Dragger blew air out through his teeth.

"In the middle of the ocean?" Chase continued to work the muscle.

He laughed. A phlegmy cackle. "Sure, that mystical location. You know there's no such place as the middle of the ocean, right?"

Chase just smiled. Her crinkly blue eyes were sunken cornflower triangles set in alabaster. Dragger momentarily forgot his pain.

"Just having some fun with you. Mind if I go deep, Dragger?"

"I should be so lucky. Sorry. Yeah, go ahead, do your stuff. I know you enjoy torturing me…" he laughed again.

"I do no such thing, and you know it." She massaged as hard as he could take it. He closed his eyes and let go a few choice expletives. Chase remained focused.

"Do you miss it much?"

"That's a loaded question."

Chase looked up from her work into his weather beaten face. Dragger's skin was like old leather, each line earned the hard way. His eyes were surprisingly gentle. And he wouldn't like you thinking that one bit. They reminded Chase of her childhood days at Gin Beach in Montauk, playing mermaid with her friends. New green seaweed plopped on their heads striking a pose in the shallow surf, legs crossed and feet wiggling like a tail. Dragger's eyes were the very same color of that seaweed. Verdant.

"Chase?" Dragger was staring at her.

"Sorry, I was daydreaming. So *do* you miss it?"

"Fishing? Would you miss your arm if it were gone tomorrow? Hell yeah I miss it. A bitch of a mistress that ocean. But you don't have her, you're miserable. I ate, drank and slept her. Best time of my life. That feeling don't go away just 'cause the body went south."

Chase almost felt sorry for him. Almost. Dragger Delray was not one of her charity cases. Old maybe. Beaten down? Never. This one will go out fighting, she thought. Dragger was a spry sixty-five years of age and could still spit fire. Age had not robbed him completely. "So tell me, what do retired fishermen do? I mean besides tell fish tales and dream about their mistress the sea?" Chase tapped his ribs playfully, making him smile. He still had his own teeth. That alone was remarkable considering.

Dragger was infamous for barroom brawls,

which he usually won. And started. Chase heard all the stories. "Yep, that sonofabitch could land a single punch and the guy would be out cold before he saw it coming." What he lacked in size he made up for in speed. He was fearless. Dragger didn't live on the edge; he invented it. When he was in his cups you would do better not to tangle with him. It was not a matter of beer balls in his case. He was born with a set of brass ones and a chip on his shoulder he brandished like a well-worn callus.

Dragger Delray was one of the bad boys. In his prime a girl like Chase would have stayed miles away from him. But this older seasoned version of the man whose arm she massaged three times a week didn't frighten her one bit. She rather looked forward to his appointments and their conversations. His part always peppered with choice words. The sad fact remained that Dragger was an old man with a bum arm and a bad cough. Hardly a threat to anyone anymore.

Chase wished she had known him back in the day. She was in diapers when he was a decade into his sea legs and barroom antics. Just one night. That's all she would ask for. One night with Dragger Delray in the middle of the ocean.

"Yeah, we old Saltys tell each other how we used to harpoon giants, haul 'em in and go back out and do it again. Now someone's harpooning our rear with needles and hauling us into bed or the dirt nap." He laughed hard, causing a fit of coughing. Chase helped him sit up and rubbed his back, gave him a cup of water.

"Thanks, kiddo." The coughing spasm let up.

"Still puffing away, I see?" Chase admonished him like a caring daughter.

He waved his good arm at her. "I'm gonna quit now? What's the point? So I live until I'm 90? No thanks. I'm going out with a Marlboro between my teeth."

Chase left it alone. She eased him back down on the table and continued moving his arm, testing his range of motion. "Not bad, Dragger. How do you feel about a little electric stim?" He was grinning the most devilish grin. In that moment he was ageless.

"Whatever you're offering, Chase, I'm buying."

She laughed and wheeled over the electric stimulator. She squirted some gel on his bicep and ran the wand up and down his muscle. "Keeping out of trouble, Dragger?"

"Best I can. I ain't one for sitting around waitin' to die. And if I start going to the senior center calling bingo, shoot me. Right in the head, quick. Nah, I keep busy, don't worry. You gotta, keep your finger in so to speak…"

Chase was intrigued. "Really? I know you're not fishing with this arm. And I know golf is not your game and hockey was done a while ago, yes?"

"True, true, you got me there. No, no hobby. This is a totally different product I'm involved in. Right up my alley."

Chase raised her eyebrows. "Are you dealing pot?"

He laughed. "Nope. Thing is I can't tolerate the ma-ra-ji-juana no more. Makes me see stuff that ain't there. Scary shit. Like my ex-wife. Shame isn't it? Man, I loved some good weed. Got to get my pleasure elsewhere. That's why I come here three times a week. Whatever you're doing feels amazing, by the way."

"At your service, Dragger. So no home grown and no hooch? Doesn't make this Jack a dull boy apparently."

"Hah. Good one. Speaking of Jack…we were joined at the hip once. I cursed him every morning my head was splitting. But I crawled back inside him every night. Couldn't quit that juice. Jack Daniels and me, we go way back…"

"Now you're squeaky clean, is it? Your days at sea and bar merely memories?"

Dragger had to laugh, which prompted another coughing spasm. Chase kept her mouth shut.

"I'm clean as a whistle. I ain't hauling as much as one lobster pot. Nope, nothing going up but my pants these days and not as often as I wish, if you catch my drift."

Chase laughed and a thrill went through Dragger. The sound of her voice like a sweet ocean breeze caressing him. In his mind he was young Dragger. What he'd give to be that young man again. He would rock Chase's world. Time is not fair.

"So are you going to keep me in suspense?" Chase followed him into the exercise room. Dragger lifted a light weight and did his reps. "What do you mean? Oh yeah, old fishermen and all that, right. Well, we marry our physical therapists, of course. You know you have great hands, Chase. Strong, but smooth and soft. Below deck hands, we call them. Anyway, since you asked, you want to hear a little story? Now that the old bat on the next table is gone…"

Chase laughed and shook her head. "You're impossible, you know that? Yeah, go ahead I'm all ears."

"Who told you that?" Dragger demanded.

"Excuse me?"

"It's not your ears men dream about, Chase. Trust me."

"Don't go there…" If the old coot mentions the word hooters or headlights or puppies or whatever crude term men used these days, Chase swore she would induce serious pain on his next visit.

"See what I mean? There it is. Your eyes. Mesmerizing. Sexy as hell. Could steal a sailor from the sea like the song goes. Honest. Kind. Rare. I oughta know. I've stared into the opposite, and it ain't pretty."

"Wow. Thanks. Maybe I will marry you. I have no better prospects, that's for sure."

"That's pathetic, if you don't mind me saying. You ain't exactly over the hill, Chase. How old are you? Thirty five?"

"If only. That ship sailed. I'm in my forty first year as a matter of fact and men my age want to date 20 year olds. Well sleep with them anyway. Vacant eyed blonde nymphets. Am I telling you something you were unaware of?"

The gal had spunk. He liked that. "I'm flattered, kiddo. You have no idea. An old fart like me. Those guys are morons, if they ain't chasing you. Men are worms. Stupid. We grow up too late and miss the boat. We don't get it. Then we piss and moan 'cause we ain't getting it. Look at me. I worshiped Jack. I woke up old and alone. I go to the john three times a night, and can't raise the johnson like I used to, on a whim. Life's a bitch. Listen, you hold out. Somebody worth your salt will come along. Otherwise I'm your man. I would be honored."

Chase cracked up. Wisdom ala Dragger Delray. Priceless. She wished he were twenty years younger. Hell, even ten would do. One thing was certain. Dragger in his prime would have worn her out. Yet she would like to have been given the chance. Lately her seas were seriously calm.

"Like I was saying, you want to hear the story or not?"

"Absolutely. I'm all ears." Chase winked.

Chapter Two

By the time Dragger finished his story, Chase was in a peculiar state. She excused herself while he finished his exercises. She poured herself a tall glass of water and closed her eyes. She had been aroused there was no question of that. And she wasn't quite sure why or what to do about it.

Chase Hooker worked hard and never complained. She even had a sense of humor about her name. She could have been named after her paternal grandmother. Henrietta Hooker. Thank heaven for small favors. She put in fifty, sixty hours a week and truly loved her job. The money was decent but she wasn't going to get rich and retire early. She had benefits and a retirement plan. A girl could do worse.

The downside was that she would likely put in twenty years of her life before she could reap any rewards and her feet were already killing her. With nobody waiting at home to rub them at night. Her social life was a non-event. She was getting too old for children if Mr. Right ever did show up. The wild oats she sowed she could count on one oat. Face it, she thought, you're boring. No one wants to date a brainy woman. A smarty pants. A bookworm. Not when sluts are a dime a dozen. Women who want to talk before they get horizontal, are high maintenance. Give a guy a hungry drunk airhead and he's happy as a pig in shit.

In the meantime Chase had her work and her satisfied clientele, mostly a bunch of old geezers with bad hips. She had a trusty stack of novels by her bed, Masterpiece Theater and a small glass of Port after her lonesome dinner. If she felt froggy she would give Mr. Vibrator a go, but lately she was too tired for even mechanical stimulation. Chase suddenly realized she had entered into the sad case zone. What would become of her?

Soon enough she would be lying on one of those black tables waiting to have her old bones massaged. Her legacy being what? Stories of hip and shoulder surgeries. The dedication she had to the field of physical therapy. How she won at bingo last week. That glimpse into the future was gloomy. She wanted to have a story to tell in her golden years. An exciting one. Was this her chance to create that story? Opportunity was knocking. Did Chase have the gumption to answer the door?

She grabbed a bag of ice for her favorite client and returned to the exercise room.

Dragger was standing by the window looking at two seagulls fighting over a clam.

Chase stood beside him. "See those birds, Chase? They know exactly what they want. Their lunch. That damn clam. Simple. They see it, they take it." He sat down in the chair and Chase put the bag of ice on his arm. "Ah, thanks, kiddo."

"Your welcome. What if I told you I know what I want?"

"Your lunch?"

Chase laughed. "No. A change. A trial run at least…on my days off. What do you say?"

Dragger was caught unawares. "Sit down." He motioned to the chair opposite him. Chase was happy to get off her feet for a moment.

"You serious?" Dragger had to catch his breath on this one. "It was a story, Chase. True, but I didn't mean to …Christ, what the hell is the matter with me? You got a good thing here. Honest work. You'll find a good guy and settle down and maybe have one of those little brats to spoil. Nothing wrong with that scenario."

"I want to know if you'll hire me, Dragger. Spare me the rosy future glimpse, please. I read all the fairytales. They're lies."

Dragger scratched his head. Maybe he should put the ice there instead. It could aid in his thinking. Or on his johnson, because that's where his brains were. How was he supposed to respond? Chase was a nice girl. Woman, he corrected himself. In any case, she deserved a fair answer.

"In a heartbeat, kiddo. One one thousand, two one thousand, three… you're hired." Then in a whisper, "Got any sexy clothes?"

Chase smiled. "I can clean up real nice, you'd be surprised."

"No doubt in my mind. No doubt at all. What time do you blow this pop stand?"

"*Tonight*? You want me to start *tonight?*"

"Settle down there, kiddo. I meant dinner. Seven o'clock. My place. I know you eat fish. I got some fresh fluke on ice. Hey, by the way, you dance?"

"Jesus, Dragger. What? Like on a *pole*?"

"Whoa nelly, you got some imagination. I meant a little foxtrot to Sinatra."

"A what?"

"Never mind. We'll mambo to the Gypsy Kings. That better?"

Chase laughed. "Much. Can I bring dessert?"

"I won't say no. Make it chocolate. I got a mean sweet tooth since I buried old Jack. Speaking of which, if you want some wine, bring it. I don't keep it in the house. Temptation. A drunk's only a drink away and all that jazz Bill W taught me."

"Coffee will do for me. I'm kind of a caffeine addict myself. And chocolate is my middle name."

Dragger laughed. "Chase Chocolate Hooker. Sounds like a porn game."

"Then I'm headed in the right direction, I'm thinking…born for the job."

Dragger shook his head and stuck a Marlboro between his teeth. "We're gonna get along like clams and horseradish, kiddo." He pushed the door and lit up as soon as he hit the salt air. Chase waved goodbye and looked up at the clock. Four more hours until her sea change.

Her next client limped in and she helped him ease himself onto the table. "How's the arthritis, Joe?"

"Like you Chase, always there."

"That's me. Old reliable. Creature of habit. No surprises."

"Chase? You feeling alright?"

"Don't mind me, Joe. Just having a strange day that's all."

"I'm too old for strange. Give me ordinary and I'm a happy camper. You'll see when you hit my age. Big thrill is The Star coming out on Thursday."

"I was hoping for a little more excitement, Joe."

"Then go to Vegas and dance on a table. You hang

around too many old people, Chase. We're like the living dead."

Chase laughed. Not all of you, she thought.

Chapter Three

"That was hands down the best fluke I ever ate." Chase sipped her coffee and glanced out the window at Montauk Harbor. "Some view. Beautiful."

"Yeah, not bad, huh?" Dragger wiped his hands on a dishtowel and came over and sat at the table. "Glad you liked the fish. I cooked on the boats. We all took turns. I make a mean spaghetti sauce. Killer meatballs. Big, you know, no girlie ones."

Chase laughed. "I don't think I'd ever wake up cranky looking out onto this every morning."

"Yeah, I have to say, even old cantankerous me is grateful for this place. It's small but what do I need bigger for? When my daughter and the husband visit, they stay at her mother's place."

"How is Tribeca? Or should I say Dr. Delray?"

"She's awesome. Who the hell would've thought I'd be the father of a doctor? Nobody in this fucking town, I guarantee you that. Takes after her mother."

"Don't sell yourself short, Dragger. You adored Tribeca, which has to count for something. She knew that."

"I guess you're right. Who the hell knows?"

"I do. Two parents wild about her gave her self-confidence. But she had boundaries so she wasn't a brat. Look at a lot of the kids today. Spoiled rotten and the boss of everyone and so lost, so damn lost. Eternal children. Endless drama. Coke, pills, alcohol, zero self-worth. Look around. Smart for her to leave when she did. Before some loser married her and strapped her with a brood of kids. She was so beautiful but you made sure she got smart too."

"True enough, Chase. What about you? You left Montauk. What made you come back and Tribeca stay on the West coast?"

"Tribeca fell in love with the Pacific and her husband, remember?"

"Yeah, what's his name. You come back home for a man then?"

"Nope. Some of us can't stay and some of us can't stay gone. For some reason I was drawn back out here. And one year just turned into the next…"

"You're a profound thinker, Chase Hooker. No doubt it was the best thing for Tribeca to go spread her wings. Get the hell out of Montauk. World's a big place. More perspective when you're not the big fish in the small pond anymore. Don't get me wrong, people would kill for this but it ain't all pretty postcard. There's an underbelly to the town. The walking dead. It's freakin' incestuous at times. People run out of new blood to f... well you get what I mean. There are more sharks than in the damn ocean. I always said I walked easier at sea. The fish are kinder. Once you respect the ocean, you're okay. You mess up on land, they brand you forever, believe me."

Dragger walked outside to his tiny terrace overlooking Montauk Harbor. A few late boats were heading back in. He lit a cigarette while Chase excused herself to use the bathroom. He could never leave this place. He tried. Went south, North Carolina, Georgia, saw some of the world, not a lot, but enough to get pulled back to Montauk every time. He was like a damn homing pigeon and the sea lured him to her time after time. It was in his blood. He was meant to die here by his ocean. God knows he lived hard enough on her. Dragger never did one thing in his life the easy way.

Who wants to be a boring drooling old bastard? Not me, he thought. He had his little piece of heaven, a ramshackle apartment above a bait and tackle shop on prime real estate that could never be developed. Too close to the water. His luck. And his view every day he woke up and was spared the dirt nap.

"Ready for dessert, Dragger?" Chase came outside and stood next to him. "I'd forgotten how beautiful it was up here. I used to come here with Tribeca when we were kids. Didn't Lake's parents own this building?"

"Yep. Lake talked them into renting it to me a long time ago. I wasn't fit to live with once upon a time. I ain't proud nor ashamed of it. Just was the way it was. Lucky for me, Lake didn't rub my nose in it. Tribeca always came first to both of us. Anyway, enough serious shit, let's eat some chocolate."

Chase poured them both another coffee while Dragger polished off his brownie sundae. Hard to believe this young woman was his daughter's age. And it wasn't like he hadn't known her all her life. But kids leave and when they come home sometimes you barely recognize them. Chase Hooker was all grown up and then some. Settle down, you horny old motherfucker, he chided himself. Wasn't he just saying how the town was incestuous?

"Something on your mind, Dragger?"

"Good brownie. Bakery downtown?"

"Listen, I wasn't born yesterday and I've lived here all my life save four years of college and one on the road. I already told you, no one's knocking my door down. I'm not looking for pity, mind you. So is there anything I can do for you? Don't give me that look. We're both adults now. I just figured I might as well audition at the hands of the master…"

"Well fuck me in a duck blind. Holy shit. Man, you are one blunt girl. I don't know what to say. But hang on I'll think of something real quick. I ain't one to brag but well, maybe I am. Point is I got no real problem hoisting the mast, so to speak. But I honestly didn't invite you here for that. The thought never crossed my mind."

"Thanks a lot."

"Chase, be fair now. Even old Dragger's got some morals. I am freakin' flattered. This was supposed to be business. And supper."

"Well supper's over. And your business is sex isn't it? Or did I misunderstand the story earlier? Were you lonely and just pulling my leg?"

"The truth, so help me. What exactly did you have in mind, kiddo?"

"First of all you have to stop calling me that. What kind of prostitute has a name called 'kiddo'?"

"We don't use that term. They're Mermaids."

"Clever. Call girls on a boat. Brilliant."

"I didn't invent it. It's been done before, in the Asian islands. Cheap fish, that's what they call them. We don't associate with that type of business. Our establishment is class all the way. No kids, no rough stuff. Top shelf."

"Is that another ocean metaphor?"

"Good one. Anyway, I thought you might want to let the story simmer awhile before you decided one way or the other. Take your time."

"How do I know if I have what it takes? How do *you* know?"

"That a loaded question? Listen, Chase, I can tell you got what it takes before you take a stitch off. These things I just know. What do you say we have that dance?"

"I get it. If I can dance, I can f...."

"Whoa nelly." Dragger clicked on the stereo and the Gypsy Kings tribal beat took over.

Chase felt amazingly relaxed without one drop of alcohol. She let Dragger lead her across the room. Who knew he was Fred Astaire? When she felt his hand holding the small of her back as he dipped her, gone was the therapist/patient relationship. This was strictly man/woman. Drumbeat. Bodies. Heat.

Chapter Four

She had stripped on coffee. No one was more surprised than Chase herself. Dragger was speechless until he let go a series of "holy shits." Chase had laughed it off like she did this every day. Stripped for the father of her childhood friend. Yet she felt completely at ease at the time and had no regrets.

Dragger called her a natural. He would know. Even at his age. "Did I seduce a senior citizen?" Chase said out loud, doubting herself for a moment. But it was an audition, nothing more. Well not exactly.

It happened spontaneously. They danced. Chase somehow began a striptease. The next thing she knew… She shook her head now and got up and poured herself a fresh cup of coffee. She tapped the old china cup. It was from her mother's collection. Oh my God, her mother. What would she say if she were alive? "Good going, Chase, you're not such a prude after all. How was he?" Yes, that would be her mother verbatim.

Her mother loved to shock her. She and her nurse friends loved their dirty jokes and bedside nursing tales. Their favorite was old man Seacock who was appropriately named since a regular Foley catheter would not do for him. He required something akin to a Wonder Bread bag. "I have never seen a penis that big in my life, Chase. I mean no wonder Sally Seacock was bowlegged. Can you imagine?"

"No, Mom, but thanks for the visual. Now

every time I see her walking her bike I'll be thinking of that." Her mother laughed. "That's why she walks her bike, don't you see? Poor thing can't ride after…"

"Okay, I get it."

"You have got to lighten up, Chase, or you'll never have any fun. Life is all about sex. The rest is just trim, if you'll pardon the pun."

Her mother was a piece of work. She lived for a good time and the talk be damned. How she wound up with such a serious boring daughter baffled her until the end. Chase figured the loose gene skipped a generation. Until last night. Oddly enough her mother would have been proud, and very jealous. You had your dirty stories, mother, Chase thought smugly now, but you didn't sleep with Dragger Delray.

And launch a new career to boot. I may be my mother's daughter after all.

Chapter Five

If anyone told me I would be a partner with a Sporty, I'd have denied it up and down. I have no time for sports fishermen. I'm not alone. Most commercial guys don't. Sportys are the elite. They don't fish for a living.

I don't mind the recreational guys on their small outboards fishing for fluke or sea bass and calling it a day. Sportys, on the other hand, have fancy boats and money to buy lobbyists. The fishing regulations don't necessarily apply to them. Sportys have careers on land. Saltys put food on the table. And they take all the heat for it.

From the tree huggers specifically. Young twits out of college who have never seen the ocean let alone been on a fishing boat. Making a fuss over how commercial fishermen have earned their living for as long as there was water and a boat.

Sportys don't catch half the heat. Only when they enter their big shark tournaments and net a big payoff for gaffing a thrasher and hanging it on the dock. Big shot hunter of the deep. Come Monday they're back in their starched shirts behind a desk making deals. You don't see me walking into their offices like I know what the hell I'm doing. Well the ocean is my place of business and Sporty ain't welcome. They have the luxury of mood and weather; commercial guys don't. We go out regardless. Dead of winter, miles and miles offshore. Weeks at a time. No guarantee of returning.

Shit happens. Especially on a commercial

boat. Rough weather blowing out of nowhere. One single misstep on a line and you get dragged overboard before you can say boo. The ocean takes no prisoners. She's a hard, unforgiving mistress. Poor Hank found that out. Hell we all learned the hard way that day. Poor fucker went straight down to Davey Jones, never having the chance to relish any lesson learned nor live to tell the tale. Like I always said, a half step can kill you.

We were down North Carolina trawling for giants. Two to four hundred pound blue fin. It was opening day of tuna season. About a quarter of a mile away from our boat, Hank fished alone. Don't ask me why, makes no sense to be alone out there. No good. Not hauling giants, man.

Hank was fighting his fish. Nothing unusual in that. Giants can take anywhere from ten minutes to an hour to catch. Depends. Commercial guys usually do it in less time since we have harder gear. So me and my buddy were busy harpooning our own giant when we heard fishermen over the radio calling Hank. No response. I knew that meant trouble.

We worked our way to Hank's boat, Dead To Rights. Eerie. I boarded. No life on deck. I walked to the cockpit. I saw what I dreaded most. Hank's harpoon line caught in the cleat. Hank was in the water. How long?

I started pulling up the line. I don't pray, but I did that day. Did Hank? There wasn't time. I saw the blue fin surface, still attached to the line. Then I saw Hank, attached to the giant, the line wrapped around his leg. He had been dragged to the bottom by the fish. Probably in the water forty minutes. The fish and the man died together. Fucking shame. Nice guy. I had coffee with him that morning. Met him in Gloucester some years back. The guy liked to fish alone.

There's no second chance, man. You get caught in a harpoon line; it can be a horror scene. Limbs get ripped off. You don't want to see it. The thing with Hank, nobody saw him go into the water. Shame. Bad ending to the beginning of tuna season, you know? Poor Hank. Rest his soul.

That's not to say there is no tragedy on party boats. Look at The Pelican. All those day fishermen dead. But that was the exception, not the rule. The sheer fact that commercial guys spend the better part of their lives on the ocean leaves more room for lives lost. Sportys wouldn't understand. And that's why I had no time for them. In the end turns out I was right all along.

Chapter Six

Gunther Shmidt was a cool enough guy, "For a Sporty," Dragger always reminded him. "Fuck you, Salty, you don't own the goddamn ocean," Gunther would give it right back. "Yeah but we never claimed to. It's our living, asshole. We ain't got no hedge funds or trust fucking funds, so blow me."

"I ain't that lonely, motherfucker."

And that's how it went for years. The two of them crossing paths, drinking at the same bar, trading barbs. Opposite ends of the bar at Liars. Dragger between trips holding court with the Saltys. Gunther or Grunt, as he was known, trolling the local talent. Neither expecting this night to be any different than the last. Neither one of them the wiser that of all the people in the world a tree hugger would change their lives.

Aspen Sputenridge walked into Liars Saloon and sat down on the only open barstool. Dead center within earshot of both Dragger and Grunt. Em served him a Sam Adams with her usual smile, which Aspen returned in kind. Pretty boy, she thought. Nice teeth. If you go for that Clark Kent type. Personally Em liked her men more broken in. Seaworthy. That's what she knew. Fishermen. Not men with manicures. Not that pretty boy had one, but he certainly hadn't seen the deck of a boat in his life. A tourist probably. Dive bars were all the rage.

The bartender turned her attention to the local bad boy and his nemesis. "Don't stare at me with those green eyes, Dragger, I'm onto you," she thought. The one girl in town he didn't have. And that wasn't about to change anytime soon.

As for Grunt, the with the baby blues Mel Gibson had nothing on; Em's jury was still out on him. She didn't fall for his charm either, and not for his lack of trying. Actually Mel's eyes were warmer. Grunt's had a cold streak. Something almost sadistic there. He was a big one. At least six four. Full head of dark hair. No beer gut. Worked out in a city gym during the week. Kept the two martini lunches down to a minimum. Divorced. No surprise, given he was quite at home slumming every weekend with the rest of the Sportys at Liars.

Clark Kent was ready for another beer. He bought the bar a round. "This one's with…excuse me, what's your name?" Em asked. "Aspen Sputenridge," the newcomer said. Em smiled. "No kidding? Drinks are with Aspen," she said, ringing the bell at the end of the bar. Aspen thought her charming. A nurturer. Zaftig. Mistress of her domain.

Dragger nodded to Grunt and he started chatting up pretty boy. He moved closer and the conversation went non-stop for a good hour. Em was eavesdropping. Dragger could read her thoughts. *What a trio. Three men walk into a bar…salty, sporty, and tree-hugger. What could these three possibly have in common?*

"To the tree-hugger, cheers," Grunt raised his scotch.

"Yeah, dolphin licker, salute," Dragger toasted with his Coke.

Aspen laughed. "To us, gentleman. To our venture."

Then in a barely audible voice above the jukebox, "Whore boat captains, extraordinaire."

Em heard it. She was wiping down the bar right in front of pretty boy. She raised her eyebrows at Dragger and gave Grunt a cool stare. "What's up, Em?" Dragger failed miserably at innocence. Em whispered in his ear as she slid passed to get the ice bucket on her way to the storeroom. "Need a madam?"

"*You* Em? No fucking way. What about the bar?" Dragger asked her when she returned after he picked his jaw up off the floor.

"What about it?" She plunked the full ice bucket down on the bar with one hand and unloaded four bottles of booze she had cradled in her other arm. Her forehead was perspiring. "I figure the work is easier and the pay better. Am I wrong? You know I can handle anything. This ain't exactly Bobby Vans."

"We'll talk Em. Away from here. I'll call you tomorrow. Awesome, Em."

She smiled. Dimpled sunshine, Aspen thought, listening intently. "I'd like to buy you a shot, Miss Em," he announced, beaming at her. "Is it Emily? Emmeline perhaps?"

"It's just Em, and thanks but I have one already." She motioned to a short brandy on the back of the bar. Aspen smiled. "Right then, Em."

Grunt laughed loudly. A diabolical sound, Aspen thought. "We're making history here, boys. Joining forces."

"Fucking history," Dragger agreed. "Nobody would believe it."

"Fuck 'em, " Grunt grunted.

"What do you say, tree-hugger?" Dragger asked pretty boy.

"Fuck them, whomever they may be." Aspen Sputenridge clapped the fishermen on the back, none too lightly. Okay, pretty boy's got a little muscle. That's promising, Dragger thought.

Em interrupted their laughter. "So tell me where were you planning on setting up shop?" She lit a cigarette and blew the smoke out the window.

"I'll tell you where, Em," Dragger said. "In the middle of the ocean."

Chapter Seven

Don't assume this whole make nice with Sporty thing happened overnight. The same way tuna don't jump out of the ocean and onto your pretty sushi plate. There were steps in between. Important steps. Patience. The right conditions. Sweat. Regulations. Skill. Did I mention patience? Finally a product someone wanted and was willing to pay for. The whore boat was no different. Timing was everything.

By nature, Sportys and Saltys don't piss in the same pot. Only this time it had nothing to do with fish. Mermaids didn't have to be caught. The women came willingly. They were well paid and treated with respect. Em would read anyone the riot act otherwise. That included myself and Grunt. As for Aspen Sputenridge, or Ass, as he came to be affectionately known, he was a gift. A happenstance of good luck.

Chapter Eight

Aspen Sputenridge was so named after the ski town where his parents fell in love. Lucky for him they hadn't met in Boulder. Nonetheless they raised one smart little tree hugger. He alone came up with the floating bordello idea. "It beats the hell out of writing articles nobody reads and sounding alarms to old ladies in Ohio. Beware! The commercial fishermen are killing Flipper!" It was all propaganda and Ass knew that better than anyone. There's always pressure to tell people what they need to hear. You make it up if you have to. In the end he gave it all up to be part of something that reeked of excitement and manhood. He was popular now. Aspen Sputenridge was a whore boat captain.

Who would have thought a brainiac like him would walk so comfortably in such salacious shoes? Dragger was in awe of him. The way he laid out the plans of the operation to the letter on Dragger's old kitchen table. "He's got fucking blueprints, man. Look at this. Look at the bedrooms. Not bunks, Grunt. And a salon, ain't that what you call it, Ass? Look Grunt, like in the movies. Where you meet the Mermaids. Cool."

"Exactly, Dragger. Well said. We are not a saloon at sea, rather we are a ..."

"Ferry of fornication," Grunt offered.

"A vessel of vaginas," Dragger added.

"I prefer ark of erotica. Or brigantine of bliss."

"Holy shit. That's fancy shmancy talk," Dragger whistled.

43

"You're a poet, Ass. No doubt about it," Grunt agreed.

"Thank you, captains. Proud to be aboard, so to speak."

It turns out Ass had knowledge beyond flowery verse. He knew all about international waters. And their boat need not have a flashing red beacon to lure patrons. Word of mouth would be sufficient. Among fishermen it always was.

As for Grunt, he had connections as to how long they could be at sea without arousing suspicion since they would not be hauling any catch. One hand washes the other. Grunt knew plenty of eager johns. He himself was no stranger to call girls.

Dragger, on the other hand, personally never had to pay for sex. Pussy flypaper, his buddies used to call him.

Ass admitted he had neither frequented a whorehouse in his life nor spent a second on a boat other than a kayak. "Why a floating bordello then, Aspen?" Em asked, preferring his given name.

"Well Em, to be perfectly honest, it came to me in a dream. A very vivid dream."

Em smiled. "Aspen darlin,' if you've never been, pardon my crudeness, laid on a boat, then put it on your list of 100 things to do before you die."

"Charming, Em. I suppose the lapping of the waves brings out the horny little mermaid in all of us, hmm?"

Em laughed. "Aspen, you are something."

"Or something else. May I say I find you utterly delightful as well."

"You may."

"Okay, so if we're done with Upstairs Downstairs chitchat can we get on with the plans, or were you going to serve high tea, Ass?" Dragger shook his head and lit a Marlboro. Grunt cracked up. "Yeah, we can serve scones with every blowjob." They howled over that one.
"Right. I do suppose being blown offshore has a whole new meaning then," Ass said, straight faced.
"Very good, Aspen." Em gave him some applause.
"Thank you, Em. Now have you thought about a wardrobe for yourself? After all, you are the madam of this schooner of sea nymphs."
"Here he goes again with the goddamn poetry…"
"Quiet, Grunt. Yes, as a matter of fact I have been scouring the catalogs and put in several orders already. I'm looking forward to wearing something that doesn't smell like beer for a change."

Em had been serving Saltys and Sportys in the same bar for the better half of her adult life. She listened to every joke, every fishing story for the umpteenth time and her share of pissing and moaning by anyone owning pair of testicles that pulled up a barstool at Liars. She was the den mother. She served the drinks with a smile and kept the peace. And nobody with half a brain messed with her. I saw a grown man cry outside the door begging for another chance to come inside after Em threw him out for starting a fight. Or trying to break one up, so he claimed. By throwing three stools in midair across the bar. Like a mother scolding her young, Em firmly insisted: "No. You don't throw furniture. Out. Good night. Go home." And he did. With his sorry tail between his legs.

Em would bring her friendly yet no nonsense approach with her into her new line of work. She was in charge of the Mermaids. An *irreverent* mother if you will. There would be no B to B: bar to boat, as the Saltys called it. Or in this case: boat-to-boat. The smell of fish guts would not be tolerated. The johns would hit the showers and change before they had a glimmer of hope to see any Mermaids. Bloody, chum-stinking clothes were left aboard the fishing boats. Just in case, Em had her own de-lousing station below deck and a closet of second hand men's clothes. No flies on her.

Speaking of flies, there was absolutely no liquor aboard the whore boat. Booze stayed on shore. That was a unanimous decision. No booze equaled less headaches. Drunk men had the potential to release their inner asshole. Didn't Dragger know that first hand. If Jack could talk like that lady on the syrup bottle…

Em was taking no chances. The bar owners were happy. It took no business away from them. People would always drink. Just not on the whore boat. It was for one purpose only. To get laid and laid well. Seahab with a happy ending.

Ass was intrigued. "As in rehab?"

"Yep. No liquor on commercial boats. Seahab."

"Clever, Dragger."

"I didn't make it up, Ass."

"Still very clever just the same."

The next bit of business had to do with tradition and good luck. Or some would say superstition. Em and Dragger knew it as gospel. Everyone in Montauk knew it was bad luck not to name a boat.

Grunt suggested the Ho Ho Ho. Ass said you might as well paint it red and call it Whores R Us. Dragger wanted A Little Tail. No news there.

Em didn't appreciate their creativity one bit. It looked like the name would have to come from her in the end.

"I have it," she said, "The Lily Virginia."

"The what?" Their voices came back to her in triplicate.

"Bear with me now. Boats are usually named after women, right?"

"Who the hell is Lily Virginia?" Dragger asked. "Never heard of her."

"Is that your mother's name, Em?" Ass wondered.

"No, Aspen. I thought surely the *fishermen* would get it."

"Careful now who you're calling fishermen," Dragger pulled a face.

"Is it a play on words, Em?" Ass wondered.

"As a matter of fact it is. Ready? Lily from the brass arrowhead attached to the harpoon line. Representing the penis, if you will."

"Do we have a choice?" Dragger rolled his eyes.

"And Virginia, well that is self-explanatory. What do you think? A keeper, no?"

"How about Seapussy? That's nautical. And well, apropos."

"This isn't James Bond, Dragger," Ass said. "Besides, Em has decided. I suggest we support her decision."

They all agreed it was as good a name as any. Grunt offered to buy everyone a steak to celebrate. Even Ass was excited and he didn't eat meat.

"Any other business before we go to dinner?" Em asked.

"Just one thing," Dragger said. "I had one other idea for a name. You might want to reconsider, Em. It's pretty good. Grunt, you're gonna love it."

"Let's have it," Em said, knowing she would be sorry.

"Sporty's Wet Dream."

"Fuck you." Grunt was not amused.

"Is this a private joke?" Ass looked from one to the other.

"Yeah, a bad one."

"Sorry, Grunt. I couldn't resist. Cheap shot, I know." Secretly Dragger loved it.

"You boys play nice or I am going to be very unhappy and that won't be good now, will it?"

"No, Em," they echoed in unison, like scolded children.

"Good. Then let's eat," Em grabbed her purse and the four brand new whore boat partners headed for The Dock.

Chapter Nine

If Ass was the brains and Dragger the brawn, though he preferred sex expert, than Grunt would be at the helm. There could realistically only be one whore boat captain. Dragger had the bum arm from a life of long lining and dragging. Ass was not what you could call seaworthy. Grunt it was by deduction if not popular vote.

The Lily Virginia would be anchored during most of her activity, which would of course take place below deck. If the captain needed forty winks or a break, Dragger could certainly take over for a time, no problem. Not like they were fishing out there. As for the Mermaids, they would change shifts when the boat docked inside Montauk Harbor. Once a week. The precious cargo would be unloaded off hours as not to arouse undue suspicion.

The Lily Virginia was not exclusive to fishermen though that was Dragger's original intention. He wanted it exclusively for the commercial guys. They fished hard, they deserved a little pleasure amidst the dangers offshore. Grunt disagreed. "Why should the whore boat only be for Saltys?"

Ass was the voice of reason in the end. This was a practical business, he pointed out. "What little boy didn't dream about finding a Mermaid? Now they get to live out that fantasy. Let's not limit our client base, gentlemen. All fishermen welcome."

Ass went on explaining how the three represented a diverse trinity, a Salty, a Sporty and tree hugger united. Unheard of. "We're making history. Do your realize this?"

"Yeah, we're the trident, man. Neptune, Poseidon and Oceanus," Dragger said.

Dead silence. "Believe it or not, I actually read a book now and then."

"Excellent, Dragger. Brilliantly put. Now where were we?" Ass went on. "Right. The unification of our individual talents and experience. What about the local authorities? Is this a concern at all?"

"The boys in blue are gonna want a taste so they won't be bothering us, don't worry. This is high class, not bargain basement bangs in some illegal wetback flophouse that screams bust me."

"So much for reading books..." Grunt said.

"Bite me." Dragger flipped him the bird.

"Ahem, *gentlemen*, as Dragger so *descriptively* put it, we must stand out from the rest without calling attention to ourselves, yes? Prostitution is still illegal," Ass reminded them.

"Then we go to the top and offer our services, free of charge. Not a problem. I can cover that," Grunt waved his hand.

"Leave it to you to know whose wheels to grease."

"Careful, Salty, you're turning green with envy."

"Attention, sea gods. Unity, remember?" Ass folded his arms.

"What about the Coast Guard?" Ass inquired.

"Coastie? The only thing lily white about them is their dress uniform. Nah, coastie's gonna want in, I guarantee it." Dragger swallowed the rest of his coffee.

"Right, then. So that leaves us with our final but most important endeavor," Ass declared.

"Finding Nemo?" Grunt asked.

"Good one." Dragger had to give him that.

"I have my moments," Grunt smirked.

"Yeah, I heard you were a one minute man," Dragger fell over laughing.

"Fuck you."

Ass shook his head. "*Gentlemen*, please. We were discussing Mermaids."

They gave him their attention. Ass went on. "Right, where will we acquire the ladies?"

Grunt had the answer. He knew someone who ran a top shelf escort service in the city. She would be happy to provide them with all the girls they needed. They could go in and pay a visit and check the girls out for themselves. Sample the merchandise. Naturally, Dragger was all for it. Ass thought it a splendid idea. Em would take their word for the actual performance, but she would check the girls' vitals. Make sure they weren't pill poppers, thieves or mental patients. Or freaks. No piercings. Em had standards. She wanted clean, old fashioned, gorgeous hookers. Grunt said that's what she would get in spades. Dozens of them. "With pussies as sweet as cherrystones on the half shell."

"Why Grunt, I do believe you are a poet yourself," Ass remarked.

"Thank you, Ass."

"So when does the tail, excuse me, when do the *Mermaids* arrive?"

"I'd say after all is said and done, Dragger, our maiden voyage should set sail at the next full moon.

Em tells me it's good luck," Ass said. " I agree. Any objections?"

" Nope. Sounds just like Em. Where did she get that one? Her psychic advisor?" Grunt laughed.

"Popeye," Dragger said.

"You sure it wasn't Bluto?" Grunt cracked himself up.

"Not the cartoon, idiot. Her grandfather. They called him Popeye. He had one bad eye. He was superstitious but he knew boats and he knew the water."

"So tell me, did Popeye ever veer from his beliefs? Like go out on the waning moon?"

"Matter of fact he did. Once. Took on water in the Rip. Boat went down quicker than my ex-wife. Anyway, they never found him. Only a piece of the boat with the name. The Emory Ann."

You could hear a pin drop in the room. Finally Ass spoke up. "Our Em. How tragic. Poor Em."

"Shit, Dragger. Sorry man, I didn't know," Grunt shook his head.

"Em doesn't talk about it. Only the locals know."

"Well we must honor Popeye for Em and set sail as planned," Ass decided.

"No argument here."

"I'm in," Grunt agreed.

Chapter Ten

"Just how long have you had it, Dragger?" Chase asked her favorite client at his next physical therapy session.

"The boat of ill repute?"

"Yes. I mean how is it no one shut you down?"

"We've been at it for fifteen years give or take. Why would they bother us? We ain't hurting anyone. And *they* are some of our best customers. Listen, Chase, men are gonna screw around. Nature of the beast. Except usually it gets complicated. Somebody falls in love. Gets clingy. Makes ultimatums and lives get wrecked. Our way, they take a little boat ride, get their rocks off, excuse my French, and no drama."

"Sounds so matter of fact. Base. Animalistic. Chauvinistic."

"Easy there, kiddo, don't take it out on my arm…"

"Sorry." Chase eased his arm back to the table.

"You're a romantic, kiddo. Nothing wrong with that. Imagine you're aboard a pirate ship dressed in all those petticoats. Queen of the wenches. Or a captured princess. Fantasy sells for a reason. Don't tell me you never read one of those bodice rippers. Well this is that fantasy come to life. Plus it pays well. You getting cold feet?"

"No, I'm not. But the world's oldest profession has a different perspective from a woman's standpoint. Is cheating not cheating if a man pays for it?"

Dragger blew out a breath. "Let me put it this way. A guy goes home and tells his wife he slept with another woman and by the way he thinks he loves her. All hell breaks loose. The fucking house, excuse my French, comes down after that bit of soul bearing. Down. Most times beyond repair. Get the wrecking ball, the game is over. Well the whore boat ain't breaking up homes. As long as Mr. Jackass keeps his mouth shut. That's why nobody's shutting us down."

"So betrayal is okay if you're fucking a prostitute?" Chase whispered the last bit.

"Mermaid," Dragger corrected.

"You're splitting hairs."

"Look, there's no emotional attachment on anyone's part. It's business, not a relationship. Not an affair. The heart stays out of it. We provide a service. We're not the moral police."

"Point taken. Why haven't I heard of the boat before? I heard no talk and this town has a big wagging tongue. The rumor mill alone could put LIPA out of business."

Dragger cracked up. "Good one, kiddo. Listen, were you in the market for a Mermaid?"

"What? No…"

"How long you lived in Montauk, Chase? Come on. There are things that go on quietly. Worlds you don't live in. Everything ain't advertised. People can look the other way when it serves them. The only illegal thing we're doing is the obvious. But there's no booze, no drugs and no fish."

"Just *Mermaids*?"

"Exactly. And a supplier knows his customers. Besides Montauk ain't no bible thumping town. Even the holy rollers on Sunday like to wrap their jaws around a cocktail or two after their sermon du jour. And that ain't all. It's a wonder the communion wafers don't catch fire on the tongues of some of them flapping fishwives. And I ain't just talking about the women."

Chase laughed. "No doubt. So tell me, why do you need a whore boat if this is hardly Victorian England?"

"You ever read Lady Chatterley's Lover?"

"Touché."

"The point is, kiddo, why do you need the cinema in East Hampton? More than one movie, right? More fish in the pond. The pond's small out here. Do I have to tell you? As far as the whore boat goes, necessity was the mother of invention."

"Not enough fish to go around?"

"Yep. And that was literally true for us Saltys. You know what a pirate is?"

"Is that a trick question? Hold that thought, I'll be right back." Chase went to get ice for Dragger's arm. She put his arm on a pillow and set the ice on his arm.

"Thanks. I ain't talking skull and crossbones and buried treasure. This is about modern day pirates, supplemental income. It happened all the time on the boats. We couldn't make a decent living anymore with all the regulations. We threw back perfectly good fish because we were over our limit. We hid the fish in a box and sold 'em anyway on the sly. To certain restaurants, etc. The way the government was pounding us, nobody was gonna eat. We learned to adapt. Secret pirate ways."

"That doesn't sound so bad."

"No, maybe not. You do what you gotta do. There was other stuff that went on. Probably still does. You choose your level of risk."

"Sounds dangerous."

"Life's risky, kiddo. Then you die."

"So where do I fit in this world? The Lily Virginia I mean. What am I? Fresh meat at midnight?"

Dragger laughed. "You got a way with words, kiddo. But no, first of all you're nobody's *meat.* Get that straight. You're a beautiful woman offering your talents. To which you will be handsomely rewarded. Don't make it more than it is. What you do aboard the boat is your prerogative, if you choose to become a Mermaid. You call the shots. But if you want to stay here doing what you do, which is excellent by the way, no shame in that."

"No money either."

"Touché."

Chapter Eleven

"Em, I have a confession to make." Chase was sitting in Em's office on the Lily Virginia. Tomorrow night she would take her maiden voyage as a Mermaid.

"Don't tell me, you slept with Dragger." Em did not look displeased. Chase released her breath. "Oh my God. He told you?" Chase wanted to crawl under the desk and hide.

"Jesus, Chase, I was born a few days before yesterday. Dragger didn't have to say a word. Call it instinct. He wouldn't by the way. Say anything. He doesn't brag. Doesn't have to. So you interviewed for the job, did you? Have fun?"

Chase was turning three shades of red, she could feel the heat in her face.

"Wow, Em, you're good. And well, Dragger was…a very good dancer." They both laughed out loud. "I imagine you impressed him yourself. A little striptease, perhaps?"

"Em, are you psychic? How the heck did you know?"

"Wild guess. How about a little performance for me now? I am after all the final say in hiring the Mermaids. I have no doubt about you, by the way. Why don't you just humor me?"

Chase felt more than uneasy. Was Em not exactly thrilled that Chase and Dragger did the horizontal mambo? Was there a jealously issue? A territorial side to her that Chase was unaware of? Maybe Em had an edge after all.

"You want me to dance for *you*? Now?" Chase

looked around the office.

"The door's locked. No one will disturb us. Hang on, I'll turn on some music."

"Um, Em?"

"Do you want to be a Mermaid or not? Shyness is not going to fill your purse, Chase. Maybe I was wrong about you. Dragger too. Look if you're not ready to…"

Chase never let her finish her thought. She was up on the desk by the time Em flipped on the stereo and walked across the room. Chase's long skirt was hiked up, flashing just enough thigh to keep the show interesting. In one smooth motion, Chase undid her zipper and her skirt fell. She stepped out of it very ladylike and quite unladylike, kicked it off the desk with her boot. She had forgone tights that morning so she shimmied, teased and turned in her royal blue thong and started to reveal her matching lace bra as she slowly and seductively unbuttoned her blouse not missing a beat.

Em was transfixed. Who knew? Chase Hooker was a natural. You would have thought she already did this for a living. Or at least kept pretty busy bedding the local talent. But Em knew that was not Chase's story. She did not sleep around. Isn't it always the quiet ones? Watching her gyrate and lose herself in the dance, no trace of shame, Em was pleasantly surprised. Chase Hooker was smoldering underneath her proper demeanor. Em didn't have a lesbian bone in her body and she was nearly breathless.

Chase was naked now except for her

cowboy boots. Em could smell her perfume. Patchouli? Chocolate? What the hell was it? It was amazing. Like Chase herself. Em was speechless. Chase jumped down off the desk and straddled Em in her chair. "Want a ride, baby?" Chase whispered hotly in her ear. Em could feel the unleashed passion through Chase's hot skin. Lucky for Dragger she didn't kill him. Fitting way for him to die anyway, she thought.

"Get off me right this minute. Jesus Christ, Chase, before you convert both of us to the other team." Em was laughing and clapping and there were tears in her eyes.

"Holy Hannah." Em took a long drink of water. Put her hand to her cheek.

"I was okay then? You approve I take it?" Chase was enjoying herself.

"May I just say in plain English, you got me wet and I like men. Speaking of which, Dragger must have gotten on his hands and knees when you left that night. And that man doesn't pray. Good show, Chase. Bravo. You are totally hired. Tell me, where did you learn to strip like that?"

"Mama. She had a lot of boyfriends after daddy died. I used to spy through the keyhole after she put me to bed. Mama would drink her two glasses of Lancer's Rose and the show would begin. I have to say, I'm a hell of a lot better and I stripped on coffee. Twice."

Em laughed. "As I recall your mama didn't have that body either. About a small wineglass full is about right, yes?"

"Yep. I inherited these girls from Granny Hooker.

Mama said she could have fed eight more kids with those udders." Chase laughed. "I figure I've got plenty of sucking time left. Not necessarily from babies…"

Em laughed. "You're killing me, Chase. I had no idea you were such a bad girl.
I have a feeling you are going to be our star Mermaid."

"I'm flattered, Em. Suddenly I am so ready for my first customer. I kind of shocked myself. Who'd a thunk I had a stripper's soul? Mama always called me a prude."

"Your mama was wrong, Chase. You are gonna knock 'em dead."

Chapter Twelve

Grunt was breaking more than one rule. He downed the rest of his Ketel One and slid the picture back over the peephole. So Em was hiring a new Mermaid. Grunt would have to break her in himself. Dragger, that old fuck had to do her first. Thorn in his side. Grunt hated sloppy seconds. No matter, he would show Chase Hooker how to get it done. And she'd be grateful. The Mermaids always were.

He put the vodka in his desk drawer and locked it. He preferred Jack but Em wouldn't smell the vodka. He'd have to thank Ass one day for his impeccable designing. Putting Grunt's office next to Em's had built in privileges, he laughed to himself. He had a bird's eye view of every piece of Mermaid ass that graced Em's office. Including Em herself changing into her madam clothes. Speaking of Em, wouldn't she just have his tender parts in a sling if she found out? He grimaced, rubbing his groin. His erection nearly disappeared just thinking about it. Luckily he was popping Viagra these days. Like a bull I am, he thought. He could give it to Chase Hooker and Em and have plenty left over for a Mermaid or two.

He should be worrying about Dragger more than Em. If he found out Grunt would be up shit creek without a paddle. Of course Dragger did have that bum arm. Not as formidable an opponent as he used to be. And Ass probably couldn't even make a fist. No, his secret was safe and he planned on keeping it that way. Right now his mind was on fresh catch. Chase Hooker was in the next room and she was about to have her informal debut as a Mermaid. Grunt wondered if she knew how lucky she was about to become?

All he had to do was wait until Em left the boat. She was like clockwork. When the Lily Virginia was docked, Em took care of Mermaid business in her office. She then headed for home, took a bath and packed a bag for the trip out that night. That gave Grunt plenty of time to do what he needed to do. Prepare for the trip, nap, break in a new Mermaid. He was getting excited. Especially after that strip show. Grunt removed the picture again and slid the peephole cover aside. He turned a button and Em's voice came into the room.

"Chase, why don't you let yourself out when you're done filling out the medical forms, okay? You can leave them on my desk. I need to pack for tonight. See you tomorrow. Nice work. Don't worry about the door, it locks by itself."

Grunt smiled. Clockwork. He heard her pass his door. She wouldn't bother him because it was his naptime. He watched Em walk off the dock and head for the parking lot. Showtime.

"Just a minute," Chase stood up to answer the door. Maybe Dragger was on board.

"Hi. Em's not here. I'm Chase. Can I help you?"

Cold blue eyes undressed her. "Gunther Shmidt, at your service." Grunt bowed dramatically. "And you are the new Mermaid." He smiled.

Chase had the urge to bolt right then and there but then she realized who he was and let down her guard.

"Not officially. You're the captain, right?"

I ain't the Easter bunny, sweetheart, Grunt thought. "None other. And if you're finished here please step into my office and we can begin your Mermaid orientation."

"Sorry? My what? Em didn't mention anything about that."

"Did she not? No worries. Our Em is a busy madam. This way, love. I don't bite…"

Grunt made a sweeping motion with his hand and unlocked his door.

Chase walked inside his office. When the door clicked shut she felt a shudder go through her. Something was not right. You're on a whore boat, Chase, not a Disney cruise. She talked herself into relaxing. "I'm not sure what I need to do here, Gunther."

"Call me Grunt. Everyone does. Relax, we're all friends here. Have a seat. Drink?"

"No thanks."

" You might reconsider. You see, before our Mermaids have their opening night, we like to give them a dress rehearsal. I'm sure Em had her own ritual for you, no?"

"Well…yes. I sort of auditioned for her. She said I was good to go."

"She meant it too. However, Em cannot do what the clients will be expecting now can she? In other words, the true test is how you measure up in a man's eyes. Your johns will be men after all. Yes?"

"Yes…but what if I told you that I was already cleared in that area? If someone told me I passed with flying colors for instance." Chase wanted the hell out of there. She did not like this Gunther or Grunt or whatever the hell he called himself.

Grunt laughed. "Dragger gave you your sea legs is it? How nice of him. He should have told me. He doesn't like to share. Since he didn't, I have to make sure you are qualified myself. You do want to be a Mermaid, yes? You can leave if you've changed your mind."

Chase knew that was her cue to bolt. But what if she caused trouble for Dragger by offending the captain? This Grunt was obviously in charge of the whore boat.

Choose, Chase, choose. Back to the boring 9-5 or become a Mermaid. Whatever it takes.

"I'll have that drink, Grunt."

"That's the spirit. Good Mermaid. Vodka okay?"

"Fine. So, do you want me to dance?" Chase took a healthy swallow of vodka.

"No need. I already saw that performance. Very nice, by the way. No, what I had in mind was more of an oral test. If you do real well with that, we'll move on to your flexibility talents."

He saw her strip in Em's office? How? The portholes were covered and the door was locked. Chase took another sip. "You want a blowjob?"

"Good, Mermaid. Now take out my cock and get to work." His eyes were more than cold. They were reptilian. Chase obliged him. She wasn't going to be in love with her johns either. She might as well learn how to detach.

"Enough, Mermaid. Take off your clothes and show

Grunt how you ride, captain ride..." he laughed.
Chase didn't. She obeyed.
"Harder, Mermaid. Don't hold back. Here, hang on
to these while you ride..."
Grunt hit the wall behind him and two leather straps
released from the wall.
Chase grabbed the straps and fucked the fucker like
her life depended on it.
"Make a little noise, so I know you're alive,
Mermaid." He squeezed her breasts beyond any
realm of pleasure and she wanted to spit in his face.
The straps were digging in to her wrists. "I don't
hear you, Mermaid."
"My name is Chase."

Grunt had a fit of laughing and took her
hands out of the straps. Thank God, that's over,
Chase thought. His eyes narrowed. "Your name is
Mermaid. Don't forget it." He roughly held onto her
arm. "You're hurting me. No more, I want to leave.
This isn't right. No one knows about you, do they?"
"Shut up. You are a Mermaid. Do as you're told.
You're not done. Kneel, Mermaid."
"I think I've had enough, Grunt. I don't plan on..."
"You don't plan on what, doing what men pay for?
You don't get to choose. Kneel, Mermaid." Grunt's
voice boomed in the room. "Here, drink up, first."
Chase downed the rest of her vodka and pulled
away. "No, no more, Grunt. I am not a Mermaid. I
don't want you to..." For a second she saw herself
running from the cabin, from Grunt's meaty hands
all over her. Then everything went fuzzy and dark.
She felt a hard crack on her backside. Another.
"Wake up, Mermaid. I'm spent. Nice ass. Virgin

territory, huh? Not anymore. Let's get you in the water..."

Chase tried to move but her body was sore. Her head ached. What had Grunt done to her? She must have passed out. What was in her drink?

"I, um, help me, please, I can't move…"

"Up and Adam, Mermaid," Grunt dragged her to her feet. Her legs were wobbly, her inner thighs sticky and wet. Her rear was throbbing with pain.

Grunt picked her up and carried her to another room and plopped her in a bathtub. He dunked her head once. Chase flailed and sputtered.

"Are you going to drown me, now?"

Grunt laughed again. "No, Mermaid. Plan to clean you up and release you. Good work, by the way. Consider yourself hired. And keep your mouth shut."

She closed her eyes. Grunt clapped. "Wakey, wakey, Mermaid. Time to swim ashore. Give us a good look at those nice sea udders first and then you can go."

Chase stood up in the tub. Her head swam a bit. Grunt grabbed her arm. "Steady, Mermaid."

Look all you want, you horrible man. If I had a knife right now, this little Mermaid would slit your throat.

Chapter Thirteen

Chase walked down the dock with a vengeance. She wanted a shower, her bedroom, a bottle of wine, heated up mac and cheese, Lifetime and a quart of chocolate chocolate chip. She would unplug her phone, turn off her cell and stay put for a week. She had grocery shopped so the pantry and freezer were stocked. She had taken two weeks vacation time from her physical therapy job to become a Mermaid. The name made her shudder now. She would tell Em she had come down with the flu. Bad timing but what could she do. She thought about Em and wanted to cry. Her eyes started to mist and she almost lost her footing. She never saw the person coming toward her. She walked smack into Aspen Spuntenridge.

"Oh, sorry," she said, dazed. Who are you? "I didn't see you…" Chase was in tears in seconds.

"Quite all right. Are you okay? Silly. Obviously you're not a' tall. May I help? My boat is right over there, the Lily Virginia. Would you like to come aboard and I'll make us both some Earl Grey?" If Ass didn't know better he would swear he had just offered the woman an hour of torture not a cup of tea. She had terror written all over her face.

"You don't like boats then?" How beautiful her eyes were. Cerulean. And her skin was like fresh cream. She was in a word, lovely. Who would dare sadden her heart?

Chase stared at him. Tea? Did the guy say he would make her *tea*? Had she stepped through the Looking Glass? "I don't like *that* boat, no. Never mind, I need to go…"

"No tea, then? And what have you against the Lily Virginia?"

"I'd rather not say. It's your boat, you said? Who the hell are you?"

"Aspen Sputenridge, at your service. Has someone aboard our vessel offended you? Grunt perhaps? He can be very off putting at times. A bit pompous. Condescending. Are you a new Mermaid?" *Impossible. Please say no.* "Did big old Grunt scare you? His bark is worse than his bite. Did our captain frighten you away? He can be insensitive, no doubt. But we cannot have our Mermaids in tears. Won't do. Not a' tall."

Chase wiped her tears with Ass's handkerchief. She looked into his kind grey eyes. "Your captain raped me. Drugged me, first. Well he wouldn't call it that. He'd call it Mermaid orientation. I could have left his office in the beginning. I didn't want to make trouble for Dragger. Or Em. He said it was what was done… that all the new Mermaids. But then I changed my mind. He wouldn't let me leave."

The woman was crying again. Ass was becoming undone.

He kept his composure. The woman was upset enough. Beautiful, but very upset.

"Okay, Miss…"

"Chase."

"Chase, I will escort you home. No point going near the boat. Please allow me to do this small gesture for you. I cannot let you drive in your state of mind. As owner of the Lily Virginia, you have my word this defilement you have endured will not be tolerated. Have you tea at home or shall I stop for some? And a tin of biscuits perhaps."

Chase looked at him. Was he kidding? Yet for some reason she felt safe. "I have plenty of tea. And cookies. Thank you, Aspen. I do feel a little too shaky to drive."

Ass put on the kettle while Chase took a shower and got into her pajamas.

She told him there was no reason to call the police or go to the hospital. She was a big girl and she willingly went into Grunt's office and performed as a Mermaid. She had planned to begin work tomorrow night. She was not looking to make any trouble for the whore boat, she explained. Ass thought it unnatural that word coming from her lips. A travesty of major proportions had taken place. For all Ass knew this behavior of Grunt's had gone on for quite some time. *Mermaid orientation my foot.* He shook his head. His job now was to comfort this beautiful woman. The rest would be dealt with in a timely fashion after a private consultation with Dragger and Em.

Chase found Ass sitting at her kitchen table. "Thank you, Aspen. I feel better now. You don't have to stay."

"Tea first, Chase. And a bickie. It will right the world if only for a moment."

Chase couldn't help smiling. "Are you English, Aspen? Or is it Irish?" *Are you real or have I imagined you?* Chase sat down and sipped her cup of Earl Grey. She studied his face. Fair skin, soft hazel eyes, black lashes, long wheat colored hair pulled back in a ponytail. Aspen wouldn't swat a fly. How could he know an awful man like Gunther?

"My grandmother was from Surrey," he said. "She minded me while my parents were off on their scientific explorations."

"Are you a scientist as well? You don't look like a fisherman. You certainly don't talk like one. What could you possibly be doing aboard the Lily Virginia? Research?"

Ass smiled. "You may find this hard to believe, Chase, but I invented the whore boat, pardon my language. A far cry from my former cerebral world."

"*You're* the tree hugger?" Chase's eyes were wide. "I pictured a much older guy. Bad suit, bald head. A twitch maybe. Dragger calls you *Ass,* right?"

Ass laughed. So did Chase. "Sadly, yes." She would be okay, Ass thought. She would put this day far behind her. And with it the ridiculous idea of becoming a Mermaid. She was too good for such an occupation. She was a treasure. A pearl in an ocean of ordinary. And though she didn't know it, it was to her credit that she lacked a hard Mermaid shell.

"Aspen? Will you keep this a secret for now? I would like to tell Em myself. And Dragger. They deserve an explanation as to why I won't be coming to work tomorrow. Is that okay with you?"

"Yes, of course. However I do want you to tell me what happened earlier. When you are ready. Mind you, not for the sake of hearing a sordid story, Chase. You have my utmost respect. I just need the facts. The violation you suffered will not go unpunished."

"But I was hired to be a Mermaid. Your captain will say he was testing the merchandise. Who is going to believe me?"

"Did Grunt pay you?"

"No."

"Then you were not a Mermaid yet. And by the way, I believe you."

"Thank you, Aspen. It happened after Em left me in her office filling out forms…"

Aspen listened to her voice and watched her perfect face and thought how one day made all the difference in the world. If he met Chase Hooker tomorrow and if Grunt had not done his dirty deed, he would be the one that had broken a rule. He would have fallen in love with a Mermaid.

Chapter Fourteen

Something was eating at Dragger but for the life of him he couldn't put his finger on it. That pissed him off big time. He had come to trust his instincts over the years. It came from being on the boats. Dicey moments at sea could do that to a person. The alarm in his brain was going off, his senses on high alert. He called his daughter. Tribeca was fine. Ditto for what's his name, the husband. Even the ex was okay. That left his partners aboard the boat. And Chase.

Now the phone call from Ass. Not a good omen. Ass never bothered him with whore boat business. He took care of everything. "You're anal, Ass," Dragger liked to tell him. He felt a wave of acid reflux. It wasn't from the coffee. His gut was talking to him. The message was not well received. Something's rotten aboard the Lily Virginia and it ain't fish, he thought. He put on his jacket and headed for the dock.

Chapter Fifteen

Grunt locked his office and walked down the dock to Liars. He needed a proper drink. It had been a productive afternoon. Paperwork and pussy. The later always put him in a chipper mood. The new Mermaid had promise. A bit hoity toity but that would change. He would see to it personally. He knew Mermaids. He'd had every one of them on the boat. He always got his money's worth. And they knew to keep their pretty Mermaid traps shut. Grunt was in charge of them, he told them. Not Em. She answered to him. Whether or not this was the truth was not their concern. They were Mermaids. Their job was not to think.

Dragger didn't have a clue. He frequented the Mermaids himself. But they weren't stupid enough to complain to him. Dragger and Grunt were partners. All the Mermaids knew it. Along with Ass, who hadn't taken to the Mermaids quite as much as his partners. "He's a queer nerd," Grunt said. "Can you imagine a young guy like him not cock deep in a Mermaid every night?"

Grunt sat in Liars and drank his Jack and Coke and smiled to himself. Just for shits and giggles, he thought, maybe I'll keep that new Mermaid all to myself. My private little sex slave. He could never get around Em with that, but the fantasy was nice. The new one was some sweet meat. Pretty good for an amateur. Yeah he could get used to that on a regular basis. He was looking forward to his next session. Before long she'd be coming by his office like a cat in heat. Grunt laughed out loud. "Something funny?" the bartender asked him. "No Sin, just thinking if you locked that door, I could show you a real good time. Make your day."

Sin burst out laughing. "Don't flatter yourself, Grunt. I've had better and I can promise you I've had bigger. Go back to your whore boat. Do I look like a Mermaid to you?"

Grunt laughed. "Well you told me, all right. Sorry I asked." Your loss, bitch, he thought. At least the Mermaids know their place. He sang along with Doors on the jukebox.

"...I'm your backdoor man..." The bartender gave him a dirty look and continued to slice limes.

Chapter Sixteen

Dragger didn't need a master key. He knew how to pick a lock. Survival skills are important. He heard a click and pushed the door open to Grunt's office. He knew sporty would be at Liars. It was his happy hour. Two cocktails and Gaviola's for a liverwurst on rye. Predictable fucker. Unlike Dragger who went on his instincts. Like the one that told him to check out Grunt's office.

He looked around. The bastard was neat, he'd give him that. Too neat maybe. He sat behind Grunt's desk and let his eyes scan the room. The Mermaid in the Waterhouse painting stared back at him. It was hanging crooked. Now who's anal? He laughed to himself. He walked over to straighten it. He stepped back. The Mermaid stared at him. It was still crooked. "Hang on red," he said to The Mermaid. He took the painting off the wall to check the nail.

"Holy shit." Dragger lifted the latch and looked through the hole. Em's office came into full view. He turned the knob. Em's radio could be heard loud and clear. She never turned it off. He shook his head. "Grunt, you fucking letch, you creepy motherfucker." He hung the painting back on the wall. Crooked or straight, Dragger couldn't care less.

He sat down in one of the leather chairs across from Grunt's desk. He stretched his arms behind his head to think. "What the hell kind of game are you playing here, Sporty?" Dragger drummed the wall and wished he had a drink. The leather straps hit him in the face. "What the fuck?" He stood up. So, Sporty's got himself his own little den of iniquity, he thought. Dragger tucked the straps back inside the wall panel and closed it. He walked over to The Mermaid painting. "Tell me beautiful sea nymph, what have you witnessed?" he removed the painting and turned up the volume. Em's answering machine came on. "Em, it's Chase. Um, sorry to call last minute…I um… have to postpone my you know… tonight. Not feeling well. Stomach thing. Came on all of a sudden. I'll call you if I can, later or…thanks. Sorry, Em. Bye."

Dragger clicked the knob and returned the Mermaid to her place. His acid reflux was coming back. He wanted a smoke. He'd wait. He wanted a Jack straight up. He hadn't had one in ten years. Chase's voice was not right on the phone. Too high pitched. Nervous. Dollars to donuts, she wasn't sick at all. And what Sporty had to do with that Dragger didn't know, but the thought of it was making his gut leak. Where the hell was Ass? He was always on time. Dragger stepped out of Grunt's office and lit a cigarette. He could almost taste the bourbon sliding down his throat. Motherfucking Grunt. How am I gonna kill you without a goddamn drink?

Chapter Seventeen

Em topped off the cats dishes and water bowls. She left a lamp on in the living room and a light over the stove. SoCo and Lime hated the dark. The two fur balls were Em's children. She spoiled them accordingly. "See you in a few days, babies," she threw them kisses as she closed her front door.

She hung her Fredrick's Of Hollywood dress on the hook inside her car. Purple tonight. Em smiled. She loved her role as madam aboard the Lily Virginia. She was born for it. All those years in jeans slopping drafts to drunks, she was so ready to play dress-up. She hoped Chase felt the same. She wanted her to feel at home on the whore boat. Just like the other Mermaids. Except she wasn't Em's usual Mermaid. She wasn't a pro. Chase was going to have to learn how to transcend and detach. She could be a top earner; she had serious potential. And a body that wouldn't quit and a face you don't find in a whorehouse. Not that Em's Mermaids weren't stunning. But they had a certain nonchalance about them. A hardness that Em didn't think Chase could ever acquire. Nor would she want her to. Chase Hooker would always stand out in a crowd. A unique blend of sexiness and class. Understated, making her all the more alluring. Yes, if Chase felt comfortable aboard the Lily Virginia, she could very well be her most popular Mermaid.

Em had a quick stop before the boat. She turned at Second House Road. She was glad to see the car. She made a right into Chase's driveway. The house hadn't changed since Chase's grandmother owned it. Maybelle Hooker had one of the original clapboard cottages overlooking Fort Pond. Now Chase was the only surviving Hooker in town. Em laughed now at the thought of it. Maybelle would be turning over in her grave.

Em rang the doorbell. She held the velvet pouch in her hand. Her future star Mermaid deserved a good luck talisman for her debut. Not that she needed luck after her performance in Em's office today. But a little turquoise and citrine never hurt anyone. Why wasn't Chase answering? Em was about to leave when the door suddenly opened.

"Em. I wasn't expecting you…I called your office…didn't you get my message?"

"No. I was just on my way to the boat but I wanted to give you this before you started. For good luck. Jesus, Chase, what's wrong? You look awfully pale and have you been crying?" Em hoped it was a mere case of cold feet or maybe a break up with a boyfriend.

"Em, I can't work for you…." Chase blurted out.

"What? You seemed ready today. What changed since then? Oh Jesus, what's wrong?"

Chase motioned with her hand as she walked away, her shoulders shaking. Em followed her inside and closed the door.

Em hugged her when Chase was through with her story. After they both dried their tears, she got up to leave. But not before she left her with a promise.

"Gunther will pay for this, Chase. Dearly. As God is my witness. He made an unforgiveable mistake. You have my word."

Em's hands were still shaking when she started her car. She lit a cigarette and exhaled her rage. "How dare you, Gunther," she said out loud. Her mind was spinning. She hit the steering wheel so hard she hurt her hand. "Damn you, Gunther," she thought. "These are my Mermaids. How dare you touch them without respect! It is not on. How could you? Chase Hooker of all people. You dirty bastard. You can have any Mermaid any night as long as you pay like the rest. But disrespect? Rape? Not on my fucking boat. As my name is Emory Ann, you will pay."

Chapter Eighteen

Ass boarded the whore boat and looked around. Everything was exactly the same as yesterday, yet nothing was the same. So much for their trinity. Dishonor had taken place. One of them had fallen. Sunk to fathomless depths. There would be no rescue for Grunt. No tag and release. His fate was sealed.

He walked past Grunt's office. And Em's, Dragger's and his own. He knew where his partner would be. He found him upstairs, on deck, a cup of coffee in one hand and a Marlboro in the other, looking out to sea. Ass watched the smoke curl into the wind and vanish. "Dragger."

"Ass, I've been sitting here trying to convince myself why I shouldn't walk down to Liars and visit my old friend Jack. You got a good reason for me?"

Ass walked over to the rail and looked into his friend's eyes. "A drink won't change the outcome. If it would I would gladly join you in breaking your sobriety."

"Really? So this meeting's got nothing to do with our finances and everything to do with Grunt. Please tell me I'm wrong."

"No, unfortunately you are not."

"Does it involve Chase?"

"So you know the new Mermaid."

"Answer the question."

"He raped her, Dragger. On our boat. In his office. I am so sorry." Ass rubbed his pant leg nervously. There was no sound except the odd seagull and the clanging of a buoy in the distance. He wished he would say something. The vein in Dragger's neck was throbbing. It was like waiting for a bomb to go off.

"Let's have it. I got my own idea but I want to hear it from you. Is Chase okay? You know what I mean, under the circumstances. Did he hit her? 'Cause if he did I gotta find him now. Spit it out, Ass. Where is she?"

"I took her home. I found her on the dock. She literally walked into me. In any event, I could see she was distressed so I drove her home and made her a cup of Earl Grey."

Dragger looked out to sea. "Right. Then after the tea party she spilled her guts and when she was okay, you called me?"

"Yes. Exactly."

"Thanks, Ass. For taking care of her. Chase is a special girl. Woman." Dragger's eyes softened when he spoke of her.

" I saw that immediately. She is lovely."

"Indeed. Which is why I am sitting here calmly listening to you and not gutting Sporty.
Give me the worst and then we take action. Go."

Ass did his best to report what Chase told him. He didn't make it anymore dramatic than it had to be. Dragger didn't interrupt him once. He listened and smoked. Ass could swear there were tears welling in Dragger's eyes at one point. When he was finished he excused himself to get Dragger a coffee refill. He knew his friend needed some privacy and time to formulate a plan. Dragger would not act in haste.

He came back to the wheelhouse with fresh

coffee and a cup of Barry's tea for himself. "Thanks. Does Em know? It will give her great pleasure to de-ball Grunt herself. I'm assuming we would have heard something."

"As far as I know, Em knows nothing. She is due any minute. In fact she is late."

"Business as usual, Ass. For now. Do I have your word? I'll clue Em in myself."

"Of course. That goes without saying. Anything else?"

"This is all my fault."

"What? Why is that?"

"I told Chase about the boat. Why didn't I keep my fucking mouth shut?"

"People make their own choices, Dragger. We all trusted Grunt had integrity. You had every right to believe Chase would be safe on the Lily Virginia. We have a Judas aboard. But you are not responsible. Only Grunt can answer for his crime."

" He will, don't worry. People always disappoint you, Ass. It's just a matter of time."

"I don't agree. We could not go on if that was the case. I can't live that way."

"And you can live with what Grunt did?"

"I didn't say that."

"You're with me then?"

"One hundred percent, Dragger."

Chapter Nineteen

In the old days, the eighties and nineties, commercial fishing was spectacular. We stocked up and went up to Gloucester. We lived on the boat. It was June and we didn't come back until October. Small boat, me and another guy chasing around 1000 pound fish. We'd pull into port here and there, but basically we were out there on the water, doing what we do. I did that for a good while. Went out on trips to the Canyons for Big Eyes. Yellow fin. We had to come in because supplies ran out. No shortage of giants. They could go for $47.00 a pound for a 900 lb. fish. You do the math. Two weeks out at Stowagon. Sweet. Long trips. Jeffries Ledge. But all that came after lobstering.

Lobstering was one cool business, man. Dangerous, no doubt about it. That's trawling. You pull that line up with its string of traps and it's no fucking joke. No time for mistakes. The surface buoy line comes up with the traps that were sitting on the ocean's bottom. The line is all over the deck. So easy to get entangled. There were fatalities, sure. But the money was good so I stayed with it. Until the shell rot happened.

The Race was a breeding ground for lobsters. That's the racing current that roars through a four mile wide gap from Long Island Sound into the Atlantic. The current can reach up to 6 mph once a month when the sun and moon are aligned with the tide. With a wind, the current is stronger. Boats get confused and caught up in it. Disaster. The bottom is all gravel and boulders so the lobsters feast on mussels and thrive. It was lobsters a plenty and we fished it like crazy until the shell rot.

Big die-off in the Sound. Cancer of the shell. Turns black. If the lobster can molt out of it, there's a chance it can survive. If not, it dies. It was caused by pesticides in the water. Individually leached or from the mass dumping that occurred more often then I care to think about. Nobody was talking.

The Groton Submarine Base in Connecticut was a landfill in the late 1960's. It caused the water in the Thames River to be compromised. They swept that shit right under the rug. You never heard squat about it. At one point there were twice the number of lobstermen than today fishing the Race. The lobsters just ain't there. Plus you gotta have the license. It's passed down through blood. I got my brother's. Today they're conching or getting squid. But not making the money they once were. The fuel is too dear. Time had it you could fish and make more than a plumber or electrician. Those days are long gone.

There was always monk fishing. Now those are the true fishermen in my book. We learned how to fish from those guys. You use a gillnet to catch live bait. Herring. You got 4500 feet of line with 15 sections a string, 300 feet each. A lot of net on the boat; a lot of weight in the water. You can get taken over real easy. You don't monkfish alone. That ain't smart. Usually there's two to three guys on a boat. Though some guys are hell bent on fishing alone. Not the smartest thing.

Monkfish are all mouth and teeth. They

have a fishing pole thingie on top of their heads. Man, they are the ugliest damn fish you'll ever see, but the coolest. Poor man's lobster. Their meat tastes similar to lobster tails. Used to be a trash fish bottom feeder. Now it's one of the highest paying catch's out there. And there's no shortage of monkfish. If all the drama with the regulations would calm down, a fisherman could fish like he was born to do. And feed his family. Now they don't go out until August and with all the regulations they're sucking the life out of the commercial guys. It's a shame.

But it wasn't the end for us. No matter what we were catching fish. Inshore. Twenty miles off the Point. Sure they set the price and regulated the hell out of us. We went back anyway. It was our livelihood. Our way of life. The kicker is that in no other business do they tell you what to sell your product for. Our hands were tied. We had no voice. And the bottom line was everyone thought it was their fucking ocean.

Don't even get me started on Sporty. Finally now they're getting a taste of how it feels to be told how you can fish. What you're allowed to take. They blamed us. It was all politically motivated. The striped bass scare. There was no shortage then and there ain't one now. Sporty knows it. He knew it then. Listen, if sports fishermen and commercial guys ever joined forces, if we could ever see eye to eye, man that would be the strongest union ever. Nobody could touch us. There would be no special interests. Just clean fishing. American commercial fishermen are the most regulated in the world. Most of your fish product in restaurants is imported. It's ludicrous when we got fish right here to sell. It boggles the mind this logic of theirs. I don't get it. One fish a day? That's bullshit. That's why I started painting houses. I had to step away from fishing. Not by choice. The trips were few and far between. It can only get worse with the fuel prices going through the roof. No more extended camping trips, man.

Chapter Twenty

Grunt almost ruined us. Almost. He dishonored the code. Abused his position as Captain. He had to pay. This ain't Oprah. We ain't sitting around talking about it and making nice. Grunt fucked us all when he raped Chase. My original instincts were right about him. In between we had those years we nearly became friends. I don't need no friends. People only give you headaches. Keep 'em at a distance, you're better off.

I couldn't forgive Grunt for what he did. And I couldn't forgive myself for letting my guard down. The whore boat was heady stuff, man. Ass convinced us that we were this fucking trio of gods. The trinity. Yeah, right. Ass surprised me the most. I have the utmost respect for that dude. Turns out the tree hugger had a fair pair of balls on him.

And no one put him up to it. He acted alone. Was it for love? Justice? Betrayal? Fact is the whore boat would have been compromised if we had just let Grunt go. Em could have fired him. The bastard would have sung like a canary, just for spite.

Em said it was all of those things. A dirty secret that brought us all closer. We weren't about to call it quits because Grunt had an issue with boundaries. He disrespected the Mermaids. No excuse. You don't mess with the goods. The product. We were invested in the whore boat. Forget Grunt.

I didn't lose any sleep over it. I killed for a living. Not people, that's true. But I hunted. Fish, deer. Still, I wasn't in the human disposal business. It was out of our hands now. Only thing left was to dress the fish.

Chapter Twenty-One

I never had a personal beef with Salty. As far as I was concerned there was enough fish in the water for both of us. I tended to agree with him there. Don't tell him that. The Saltys were just doing their job. Why would they overfish? The product would become extinct and they'd be out of business. It didn't make any sense. Just a lot of brouhaha. Yeah, sure, there were guys who couldn't stand them (the commercials) but I wasn't one of them. Guys who freaked out when they saw lobster traps where they wanted to fish. Picayune stuff like that went on all the time. Like the freakin' ocean wasn't big enough for all of us. Like I said, that wasn't my beef. I was interested in the big money. The tournaments. Shark. Swordfish. Giants.

I came out here for a charter. Night trip out of Montauk Harbor. Viking fleet. That was years ago. Loved the place. I grew up in the Bronx, so this place out here was another world. Peaceful. Perfect antidote to city business all week. I know Salty thought he had me pegged, but I wasn't your typical suit. I felt for the small guy, the working man who didn't get a business handed down to him like I did. Don't get me wrong, I can be a royal prick when I need to be. And I have a voracious appetite for a good time. Women. Drink. I'm a big German. We like to party.

I bought my own boat. A Little Piece. Slept six. Comfortably. I mean in real beds. Not those dwarf bunks. I'm a big guy, I like to spread out. I afforded my ladies the same pleasure. I keep it at the Montauk Marine Basin. Good guy there hooked me up. He liked to party a bit himself. Ran a good tournament. Opening day was a madhouse. You never saw anything like it. Hundreds of boats leaving the Harbor at the same time. It's a miracle no one dies before they even get out on the water.

I was living pretty good when I met Salty. Pad in the city, minus the wife. Bachelor cottage out in Montauk. I was living large. Lots of local and tourist talent to invite on the boat for pleasure cruises. Orgies. I got a big appetite, like I said. The whore boat was right up my alley. By then the wife was ex and I was free to fornicate my dick off. Not like I wasn't before. All those Mermaids were like putting a kid in a candy store. And I have to admit I like putting them in their place. I am the Captain after all.

Dragger thought he was sharp. But I had it all over him. He and Ass have no clue how sweet it is for me on the Lily Virginia. I would be willing to share but Dragger, tough guy that he is, would never go for it. Not that he didn't like a little Mermaid tail himself. But the rough stuff was off limits. I hate a pussy. And he'd probably split my head open if he knew I called him that. What he don't know won't hurt him. Or me. As for Ass, I still say he's light in the loafers. Em swears not. I guess I have to take her word for it. But there's no way she had a piece of Ass.

She doesn't go for that mamsy pamsy type. I'm more her speed. She likes big men. I almost had her one night. I closed Liars with her. Fetched ice for her all night. You'd think she would show some appreciation. I can buy my own booze. What I can't do is suck my own dick. "It's not like that between us," she tells me. What's it not like? You're a woman, I'm a man. She wasn't buying it. "Let's keep it at friends," she says. What are we in high school? Who the hell did she think she was? No Pamela Anderson, let me tell you.

I bet Dragger did her. I hear he had everything in his path back in the day. The bastard wouldn't share. Tell you nothing. All those AA meetings, you'd think he would talk. Not him. And he fancied himself the protector of Mermaids. Especially that new one. Well I got news for him. She got a taste of Gunther that she won't forget. Put that in your pipe, and smoke it, Salty .

Chapter Twenty-Two

The only one missing was Ass. He lacked a poker face. "I can't do it, Dragger. I cannot look Grunt in the eye and pretend everything is normal. Please make excuses for me. The sooner this situation is settled the better. Grunt must not get off scott-free." Tough words from Ass. He wanted justice for Chase. Right on, Ass. It was admirable of him. But Dragger knew his sentiments went beyond chivalry. Ass was in love with her. As he watched Ass leave the wheelhouse, he felt two strong feelings in his gut. One was brotherhood. The other was revenge.

"So where's the brainiac tree-hugger tonight?" Grunt asked later. He and Dragger sat in the wheelhouse of the Lily Virginia. They were out miles offshore and Mermaid business was being conducted below deck as usual. Dragger was on his umpteenth cup of d-caf. He brought Grunt a fresh cup of high test. "Ass went to visit his mother." Dragger looked out to sea. It was a gorgeous full moon. *I'm so sorry, kiddo. This was your night.*

"I told you he was homo," Grunt said. "A boat full of Mermaids and he goes to visit his mommy. He's a fucking queer, I'm telling you." Dragger cupped his coffee mug with both hands. He took a long sip and lit a Marlboro. He could picture his fist connecting with Grunt's jaw. Again and again. Pummeled. Mincemeat. Pulp. He blew out a stream of smoke. Deliberate. Conscious. *Easy, man. It ain't time yet.*

"Ass ain't gay. He loves the Mermaids.

Talks to 'em all the time. They love him. You know that. Cut the shit." *Asshole. Rapist. Dead man.*

"Yeah they like him like a sister. He's their sissy gay friend. Women love queers. Because they don't have to fuck them. They're like chicks with dicks." Grunt cracked up.

Dragger coughed. This business as usual stuff was getting old.

"Nah, Grunt, you're wrong, man. I saw him kiss a Mermaid once."

"No, *you're* wrong. Mermaids don't kiss. Not on the mouth. Do everything but kiss. Surprised you didn't know that. You can pay them, they still won't do it. I learned that from a pro."

"Oh yeah? Was she a Mermaid?"

"No, she was my mother."

"Holy shit. You got a mother?"

"Fuck you. Yep, the old lady was a whore. A pro. That's why I'm so comfortable around the whores on the boat. They're familiar, see?"

You are fucked up. Soon to be FUBAR. Fucked up beyond all recognition. "We call them *Mermaids*, remember?"

"Ah, they're all whores. All for sale. I oughta' know."

"So you had a few Mermaids. Congratulations. We're all out of medals."

Grunt laughed. It was a disgusting sound. "You'd be surprised. Even the shiny new ones got a price…" he started whistling.

One good shove over the deck and Grunt would be history. Dragger had to control himself. "You got something to say, Grunt? Otherwise stick to the sad mother story. I ain't in the mood to argue."

"Since when? Don't mind me, I'm just talking. But whores I know. They'd sell their own kid if the price was right."

Dragger was tired of the conversation. "Let's leave it at you got your thing and I got mine. Sorry about your mother. Tough break."

"So what is your thing? You into the kinky stuff? You like them young? Or just breathing?" Grunt cracked up again.

"I like to dance."

"What? Fuck me. Dance? What are you queer too? Ass is bad enough. I'm outnumbered now."

" Shut up. I like a little slow dancing before I fuck. You got a problem with that, Sporty?"

"Easy. Settle down, slugger. Just so the boat don't go in a different direction. I'm not into that queer shit."

"No tea dances for you, Grunt? You know what they say? You ain't a man till you had a man."

"Don't make me sick. Let's change the subject. Where's Em?"

"Mermaid stuff. Why? "

Grunt looked at his watch. " It's about her changing time, isn't it? She's like clockwork. Anyway, take over the watch for me? I'm off for a piss."

Dragger sat in the captain's chair. "No problem, Grunt. I got it." *Fucking peeping tom pervert.*

"Need anything from down below?"

A sharp knife to slice your balls open. "Another cuppa joe. And a chocolate bar. Thanks."

"You got it. I won't be long." *I can whack off in no time.* Grunt looked up. "Some moon huh? Devil moon, my mother called it. Used to scare the shit out of me. Eerie glow to it."

"Nah, the ring around the moon is good luck, man. That's what I heard," Dragger shrugged.

"Creepy moon if you ask me." Grunt shivered. *"Beware the devil moon, Gunther. Satan likes to take little boys when the moon is full."*

"Where does he take them, mommy?"

"Home."

Chapter Twenty-Three

Grunt whistled all the way to his office. The decks were clear. Mermaids all currently engaged in their carnal calling. But no kissing. Grunt laughed to himself. *Whores, they're all the same.*

He turned his key in the lock. He was envisioning Em undressing. He quite enjoyed his little peep show. It got him in the mood to tear up some Mermaid pussy.

He hit the light switch. The room remained dark. "What the fuck?" He groped around and found his desk, felt around for the lamp. The light came on. He went directly to The Mermaid painting. "Showtime, little whore." He lifted the latch over the hole but all he saw was black. Where the hell was Em? This was her changing time. She was like clockwork. Damn. He turned up the sound. Em was talking. To who?

"I just love this new dress, don't you? Red is definitely my color. This bra barely holds me in, damn. I better take it off and change into the black one."

Grunt swore. "Why can't I see her? What the fuck is wrong?"

"What's wrong is *you*, Grunt." Grunt dropped the latch and spun around.

"How the hell did you get in here?"

"Same way you did."

"What do you want? I'm busy."

"I see that. Disappointed are you?"

"Yeah. Not that it's any of your business."

"Oh it's my business all right, Grunt. You're

not in charge, motherfucker."

"Nice mouth. Dragger teach you some dirty words?"

"I'm full of surprises as you are about to learn."

"What are you gonna do, bore me to death?"

"No, actually I thought I would shoot you."

Grunt laughed. "You and what army? Besides, you do that and every Mermaid aboard will come running. Not to mention Dragger and Em…"

"I suggest you shut up and say goodbye to the world."

"Don't make me laugh. You don't have it in you, you little…"

The room was silent. Grunt's office door clicked shut.

Chapter Twenty-Four

Dragger was dying for a coffee. Where the hell was Grunt? Dragger left the wheelhouse and headed for the galley. Em was pouring herself a cup when he walked in. "It's fresh, I just made it."

"Thanks. Nice dress, Em. Hot."

She laughed. "You think? I feel a little bit like Miss Kitty."

"Can I be Marshall Dillon? Anyway, you're much hotter than she was. She didn't have that cleavage if I remember correctly."

Em laughed. "Where's Grunt? I haven't seen him all night."

"Damned if I know. He went for coffee over an hour ago. Probably screwing a…I mean having a little Mermaid fun. You know Grunt."

"Do I? I wonder. But all my girls are accounted for. And it's a little early for him anyway. Maybe he fell asleep."

"Whatever." Dragger poured a coffee and unwrapped a Cadbury Fruit and Nut.

"It's a good night but I could have used one more Mermaid." Em looked into her cup.

"You would've had one if…it was supposed to be Chase's debut. You know why it wasn't, don't you?"

"Yes," Em said softly. "And I'm sick about it. I don't know if she's strong enough to get through something like that. Grunt's gonna pay for what he did to her."

"That's a given, Em. As for Chase, she comes from strong stock. Takes after her grandmother. The mother was a bit of a head case. High maintenance. Man eater. Chase won't fold, I'm telling you. I'll see to it myself."

Em smiled. "I hope you're right. You're crazy about her, aren't you? But tell me you didn't find out about her mother firsthand?"

"No. She wasn't my type. And yeah, I got one, so don't get cute. I see that smile.

No, I like to keep my balls at the end of the night. As far as her daughter, look I'm an old salt with one foot in the grave. Chase is a beautiful young woman. End of story."

Em laughed. "Oh really? So no hanky panky with your physical therapist?"

"I made her laugh a few times. She fixed my arm up. I cooked her some fluke. So what?"

"My dentist fixed my teeth and I didn't sleep with him, Dragger."

"What's your point, Em?"

"Chemistry. Lust. It was evident in spades. She adores you. And vice versa."

"Okay, okay. I give. We danced. Don't tell Ass."

"What's he got to do with it?"

"He's in love with her. Fell like a ton of bricks. And they're the same age. And Ass is no dog."

"Neither are you. Anymore." Em laughed.

"Thanks a lot. But seriously, Ass is good for her. He'll keep his eyes in is head. She won't have to worry with him."

"You have regrets I take it?"

"What if I do? Face it, Em. It was all about the score back then. Do I even remember half their names? All those faces, all those legs…if I wrote my fucking memoirs, man…"

"Fucking Memoirs would be the title then? When you do write them leave one name out, will you?"

"Chase? Goes without saying. What about you, Em? There's still time…"

"Time for what?"

Em and Dragger turned around. Chase was standing in the doorway. The red stilettos she was balancing on matched her low cut red dress. Her blonde curls shone in the lamplight. The flush on her face was almost feverish. But her eyes were not right. Spiritless. What the hell was she doing aboard the Lily Virginia tonight?

"Chase. I'm shocked to see you here. Are you okay?" Em knew she wasn't.

"You don't like the dress? I thought it suited me."

Dragger looked at Em then back to her. "You look beautiful, Chase," he said.

"Don't call me that. I'm a Mermaid. We don't have names."

Chapter Twenty-Five

Dragger never would have thought Ass had it in him. Tree huggers are pacifists for crying out loud. Dragger reminded himself not to rub him the wrong way. The kid must have read a lot of Mickey Spillane novels growing up. The silencer was a brilliant idea. The heads up Dragger got to go check on Grunt, perfect. Ass left him a note. Inside his Cadbury Fruit and Nut. Dragger was the only one who ate them. The plans laid out for him. How they could keep it quiet. How Grunt could suddenly disappear. How there was no room on the Lily Virginia for a traitor. A traitor to the code they had as whore boat partners. Grunt had disgraced them. Ass wanted to eliminate that disgrace.

Mostly, he did it for Chase. He snuck her aboard the Lily Virginia after Em thought she had tucked her in for the night. Chase talked him into it, he said. "She could have asked me to shoot the moon for her, Dragger. I would have." Ass, in his smitten state was not using his noodle properly. Little head in charge. Dragger could only assume Chase wasn't there when he shot Grunt, but he didn't know that for sure. Ass was vague. And Chase was not operating on all cylinders. Maybe she shot him? Nah, he couldn't start thinking like that.

Dragger was thankful for a few things the night Grunt did not die. Ass had bad aim or his conscience kicked in at the last minute. Em was not in fact in her office. Ass had rigged a recording of her voice to play at the right time. In the end, the only one to take a bullet was the Titian beauty in the Waterhouse painting.

Grunt was madder than a wet hen. Though he might have recovered from his homophobia. He had a new respect for Ass. He told Dragger as much. Dragger had one reply. "I wouldn't have missed."

Grunt would live to fight another day. In the meantime, they finished their Mermaid run and came in the next afternoon. Dragger knew nothing had been solved and Grunt on a bender wasn't going to help. His lips might get loose. There needed to be a Plan B. What that was, eluded Dragger and quite frankly gave him a migraine. He popped a few Excedrins and took forty winks on his office couch.

Chapter Twenty-Six

The rest was up to me. Ass didn't have the stomach for it. Our tree hugger was a little squeamish. Not used to the blood and guts we Saltys are. I've dressed some big fish in my day. Men? Zero. But you do what you gotta do, man. Nobody was going to jail for putting to rights what Grunt did. Fuck that. My job was to get him ready for his close-up to the briny depths.

I borrowed Grunt's boat. Not that he would mind anymore. When I was done I would loan the boat to a buddy I could trust and he would take it down south. For good. In the meantime I needed a pair of dry gloves to start my work. I figured Grunt might have a pair onboard but just in case I grabbed my buddy's off his boat before I left.

I slipped them on and felt fucking mush. Cold wet mush. People don't take care of their shit, man. This guy's gloves were always wet. You put your hand in and a minnow floats out. I guess he missed the concept of dry gloves. I threw them on the deck and looked for Sporty's. His were bone dry. The pun made me a little uncomfortable, I was dealing with a corpse after all. No time for getting spooked, I had work to do.

First I had to minimize the carcass. Small body pieces disappear quicker. Sea lice would eat the flesh to the bone. I crushed the teeth. No identification would ever be found. I dropped him piece by piece into the ocean that he hunted half his life. I was chunking Sporty. There's a bit of irony for you.

I thought I'd enjoy it more than I did. Hey, I'm not the monster here. Grunt gave us no choice. And I don't blame Ass for shooting him. If he hadn't, I would have gutted Sporty myself. Point is none of us aboard the Lily Virginia were gonna let him get away with what he did to Chase. Apparently not even Chase herself. She could have easily gone off the deep end. We realized it that night she showed up looking like Irma la Douce.

Chapter Twenty-Seven

Dragger woke up surprisingly refreshed, considering the dream he had. Amazing what you can accomplish while you sleep. They still had a major problem on their hands. Grunt. He was in fact very much alive and he had to go, somewhere. The decision was unanimous. And he wasn't going to go easy. "It all comes out in the wash," they say. The next day would prove that saying very true.

Ass drove Chase home. She would have plenty of time to reflect on becoming a Mermaid. She was obviously in shock when she decided to play dress up on the boat. Em handled her beautifully. They went off to have a woman-to-woman chat. Or madam to Mermaid as it was.

The Mermaids were packed out when the boat docked until the next trip. A little R&R for the hard working girls. Grunt headed for Liars, where he planned to get "shitfaced and lucky." The first was a guarantee. Before he left he gave Ass a piece of his mind. "I'll deal with you later." Ass just nodded at him, the way one humors a mental patient. Dragger kept his mouth shut for once in his life.

His daughter was in town. He drove home for a quick shower and met her at Manucci's for dinner. She left what's his name in California, so Dragger didn't need the Tums after their fine meal. Tribeca knew nothing about the whore boat and he planned on keeping it that way. Her father took tourists out fishing. Good enough.

She watched as he polished off a brownie

sundae with gusto as she sipped her espresso. "How's the arm, daddy?" Dragger looked up. "Fine, Doc."

"I'm serious."

"So am I. It's fine, really. Thanks for asking."

"Fine then. Peter and I are going to Costa Rica this winter."

"Who's Peter?"

"Very funny, daddy."

"Supposed to be beautiful there. Paradise. Feed him to the howler monkeys."

"You're incorrigible. Can't you say something nice?"

"Have a good time."

"Thank you. Have you heard from Mom?"

"No, why would I?"

"You live in the same town. She still worries about you."

"That's touching. No reason to though. I'm sober as a judge and quiet as a church mouse these days."

"Let's not get crazy…"

"Let's not talk about Lake then, how's that?"

"Done."

"Good."

Dragger watched her swift move grabbing the check just as the waitress dropped it on the table. He started to argue, but she cut him off. "I'm paying for dinner, deal with it, daddy. I'm a doctor, remember? My treat."

" Well, thanks. How'd you get so bossy, Doc?"

"Is that a rhetorical question?"

She left a generous tip, which made Dragger smile. The kid remembered where she came from.

Her waitressing days in the harbor. He admired that. He kissed her on the cheek. "You're okay, Doc. Nice to see you're still spitting salt water and not that fancy Napa Valley Pinot Noir."

"I'm a Montauk girl at heart. Always will be. You know that, Mr. Salty."

Dragger laughed and Tribeca's grin widened. She could always get to him with that. Her childhood nickname for him. It drove her mother crazy when she would take the salt shaker off the stove and keep it on her nightstand. "Where's Mr. Salty?" her mother would call from the kitchen. "Captain Pepper needs his mate. Not to mention this soup."

"When daddy gets home, I'll give it back."

Her mother finally gave up and bought another one.

"It's nice knowing somebody cared that I came in from the boats. I'm only sorry you worried so much and I wasn't there for you."

"Mom worried too. Give her some credit. And I was fine. I'm tough like my old man. I still have it, you know."

" Mr. Salty?"

"Yep. On my kitchen windowsill, facing out to sea."

"Wrong ocean, Doc. But I'm flattered."

"I love you, daddy."

"I love you too, Doc."

Tribeca got into her mother's old jeep and Dragger waved goodbye to her. He turned on the ignition in his truck and headed for his sugar shack in the harbor. Aside from the nasty business with Grunt, life was good, he had to admit it. "Watch out

when things are gong well," the old man always said. "Bound to be heartache around the bend."
Dragger cranked up his old Nina Simone tape and lit a Marlboro.

Chapter Twenty-Eight

Dragger didn't hear drums, but the town was buzzing by the time he got to Gaviola's for his morning breakfast blend. "Yeah, no lie, a dead body in a car in Liar's parking lot," someone was telling the owner. Dragger walked over with his coffee and buttered roll. "Joe, pack of Marlboro Reds." He turned to the guy standing next to him. "What's all this about a body at Liars?"

"No shit, Dragger, the Sporty was gutted with a filet knife. Big fucking guy, I think his name was Grant, something like that." The young Salty chewed his egg sandwich. "No, Grunt, that was it, yeah," he said, like he won a round of Jeopardy. Dragger sipped his coffee without choking. "You sure you heard right?"

"Yep. Positive. Sin told me he was there all night. Hammered. Some lady hanging all over him. They call her the Appendage. So the two of them are all hot and heavy, talking about who the hell knows what, bullshit probably, and who walks in? The Appendage's husband. She gets all mouthy with him and Grunt laughs in his face. The guy don't like that and he throws a punch at Grunt, misses, and now Grunt is hysterically laughing at him and the guy starts making crazy threats, like 'Sportys a dead man.' The more he threatens the harder Grunt laughs. Sin throws the Appendage's husband out. The wife goes with him. Sin cuts Grunt off and he leaves too. Last anyone seen of him. Till this morning."

"That's a nice story." Dragger lit up a

115

smoke.

"Wait, that ain't the end. So early this morning Sin goes out to the dumpster with the trash after she closes the bar, and there's Grunt, hanging out of his car, gutted man. You know Sin, she's tough, nothing rattles her, but seeing that …she's gonna have nightmares for years."

Dragger stomped his butt out under his boot and climbed into his truck. "Hey Dragger, you know the guy or something? You look shook up."

"I knew him, yeah. Take it slow, man." He hit the gas and headed for Liars.

He had to park along West Lake Drive; the parking lot at Liars was closed off with police tape. Dragger walked under it and went over to some fishermen by the dock, getting ready to head out. "Guess you heard?" Captain Ron said, lighting a smoke.

"Yeah. Just."

"Cops were all over the place. Finished up a bit ago. Reporter from the Star is inside with Sin. She's a mess, man. Poor baby. What a sight that must've been. Sporty was gutted like a tuna. Bled out. He pissed somebody off, royally. Personally, I thought Grunt was an asshole, but you gotta be a bit psycho to do that shit, man. It's like fucking Dexter was here." Captain Ron laughed his trademark laugh. His shoulders shook and his whole face was animated. He always reminded Dragger of Chong from the Cheech and Chong movies. That stoned sounding voice. Ronny was cool. He wouldn't harm a fly.

Dragger shuffled his feet. "You see Em

yet?"

"Nope. Why? She ain't got no love lost for Grunt either."

"No, I know, I know. I got other business with her, that's all. So, they lock anyone up?"

"Not yet, but they're looking for the Appendage's husband."

"Really? They think he did it? I mean it's possible, I guess. I heard about the fight if you want to call it that."

"Yeah, wasn't much of anything. Threats mostly. Anyway, I gotta head out, man. Say hi to Em for me. How are all the little Mermaids?"

"Fine. Coming aboard soon?"

Captain Ron laughed. "What, you want to find me gutted? Don't give my wife no ideas. I like my balls, thanks."

Dragger laughed. "Smart man. Good luck out there."

"Luck is what we need, man. The fucking limit's killing us."

"Fuck 'em, pirate."

"Yeah, fuck 'em."

Dragger avoided going inside the bar. Reporters were nosy by nature. Better to talk to Em and Ass ASAP. He had a gander at the crime scene first. The car was gone and Sporty with it. Well what was left of him. The blood was washed away, but a sticky puddle remained trapped in the gravel. Dragger shivered, his dream coming back to him. He was glad he was off the booze. Imagine blacking out and waking up to that?

A bad temper, a good bag on, and a filet knife

doesn't make for a good outcome. But still, like Captain Ron said, "You gotta be a bit psycho to do that."

Talking with Ron made Dragger nostalgic for the old days. Steaming out eight or nine miles. Fish swimming right into the feed. Simple. Nobody busting your balls. They went out and came back with fish. It ain't rocket science. Now the humps were on your back for a few extra fish. The luster was gone and for that he didn't miss it.

Chapter Twenty-Nine

Em was having a tea party. She and Chase were sipping from dainty cups and Ass was spooning whipped cream and jam onto their flowery plates. "Have a scone, Dragger, Aspen made them. To die for. Try the clotted cream."

"Excuse me, mad hatters? Grunt's dead." He sat down on a counter stool and waved Ass away. "No tea, no thanks. Did you hear me? Sporty is dead. Somebody filleted his ass and left him to bleed out. Anyone here want to make a confession?"

"Knock it off, Dragger, you know damn well none of us is capable of that," Em said.

"I know no such thing, Em. Ass shot him, didn't he? Well he tried to anyway. And missy here was all dolled up like the lady in red the other night, talking like a robot. 'Call me Mermaid...' Sorry, Chase, you were out of it, kiddo."

Chase slammed her cup down and shot him a dirty look. "So that's what you think of me, Dragger? I'm a lunatic cold blooded killer? Thanks. And fuck you."

"Easy, there, darlin,' Dragger meant no such thing, did you Dragger?"

"He raped her, Ass. She trusted him and he defiled her. He knew what she meant to...anyway, I get how it could have happened. Got out of hand. I dreamt about gutting the fuck myself."

"Dragger, you're out of line. And if you don't change your tune, you're out of my house. Apologize to Chase. And Aspen. Now." Em stood with her arms crossed. Never a good sign.

"I'm sorry, Chase. Ass. Chase, remember when you and Tribeca won that fish filleting contest?" Chase looked at him, her eyes burning with anger and hurt.

"That was years ago, and now Tribeca wields a scalpel and I massage flesh and bones. Neither one of us is on the FBI's most wanted list. What was in your coffee this morning? Jesus."

"Are you satisfied, Dragger? Not only have you insulted both of us, but you are deluding yourself if you think either one of us had any part in that macabre scene."

"Okay, so I got carried away, Ass. I'm sorry. It was probably the Appendage's husband anyway. And he's missing, apparently."

"So he took care of our Grunt problem," Em said. "And don't give me that look. We didn't *hire* him. Grunt made his own bed. Too many beds, with husbands in them. Anyway, it's done and we are worry free."

Dragger scratched his head. "Pardon me, Alice, did you smoke all the caterpillar yourself? Oh no, you shared it with the White Rabbit here and the Mad Hatter. Christ, don't you realize Grunt was our partner on the boat? People are gonna talk. Besides that, we're out a captain, remember?"

"Settle down, Dragger. What ever happened to 'Sporty's got to go' and all that? And since when do you give a flying fig if people talk? We have nothing to hide, so we hide nothing. And as for the captain problem, Em has that sorted out."

"Okay, Ass, you're right again. So what's your idea, Em? I'm all ears." He winked at Chase.

She shot him the bird. He was going to have to do some backpedaling. That was a given.

Chapter Thirty

Em had the answer. Admiral Joey Flapjaws. Dragger loved it. "Why didn't I think of that? Saltiest motherfucker in Montauk. Knows the ocean like the back of his hand."

The Admiral sold his commercial boat when the fuel went through the roof. He loved the ladies, so the whore boat would be a perfect fit. There was only one problem. How would they keep him sober enough to make the trip out and back?

Em had the solution. Keep him on d-caf, watch him like a hawk, and every night a different Mermaid would visit him in his quarters and take the edge off, so to speak. He wouldn't miss the booze so much, and they would have themselves a whore boat captain. It sounded foolproof.

At this stage, Chase had calmed down and no longer wanted Dragger's ass in a sling. But she was hell bent on proving herself as a Mermaid. Ass was miserable because he couldn't handle her screwing other men. To make matters worse, he hadn't had the pleasure of her carnal charms yet. Poor Ass. Poor Chase. She didn't really want to become a Mermaid. Her pride was talking. Ass was the guy for her. This time Dragger had the answer.

He told Ass to make Chase a proposition. Suggest she go ahead and become a Mermaid, but only if he could be her first customer. Ass would normally reject such a thing. Any talk of Chase as a Mermaid ticked him off. But Ass, being the wise Ass they all knew and loved, granted Dragger the benefit of the doubt.

"You get her to agree and then you make sweet love to her and she won't be interested in any john on the boat. Dig?"

"So in essence, we are tricking her? But for her own good. And mine, of course. Thank you, Dragger, you're not all bad. I owe you one."

"We're even, Ass. You just take care of my girl. She's special."

"I knew that the minute I laid eyes on her. No worries, I'm the man for the job."

"Good. So go get busy."

Ass laughed. "You are ever the wordsmith."

"I'll take that as a compliment, Earl Grey. I do have one burning question."

"Shoot."

"Well, that's the question actually. Where did you learn to shoot?"

"Grandmother. She loved a good skeet shoot and a Pimm's Cup afterwards."

"That's a drink, right? Not a cup of tea?"

"Gin. Grandmother wouldn't be without it."

"You're a fucking enigma, man."

"Hardly. Though I must tell you that grandmother left her entire estate to me. Chase, should she have me, will be quite comfortable."

"That so? Then why the whore boat, Ass? You got it made already."

"Grandmother taught me something else. 'Have a juicy chapter for your memoirs, Aspen dear. You're a smart boy, but you could do with a little spice.' "

Dragger laughed. "I like Grandma. What was her name?"

"Everworth Sputenridge."

"Anyone in your family have a normal name?"

"You mean like Dragger, for instance?"

"Touché. You're all right, Ass."

" Thanks. Now excuse me while I get *busy*."

"That's what I'm talking about."

"Right. As Grandmother would say, 'Chatter is cheap, Aspen. Action is what drives the day."

"Grandma was one cool lady. You should name your first kid after her."

"Now that's putting the cart before the horse, no?"

"Food for thought, that's all I'm saying."

Chapter Thirty-One

The Appendage's husband was arrested. He didn't get far. There is one road in and out of Montauk. Locals know about the dirt road off Navy Road that goes over the railroad tracks all the way to Hidden Lake. Past Dog Shit Alley. It won't get you out of town, but it might buy you some time.

The Appendage's husband drove down that road like a man possessed, dove into the lake, swimming like the clappers for the duck blind on the far shore. He could hide out there for awhile was his plan. What he forgot was the lake was inhabited by some mean snapping turtles. One hungry reptile clamped onto his arm and he let out a scream that echoed around the lake. Some hikers heard him and called for help on their cell phones. Good Samaritans are in the unlikeliest places.

The Montauk Ambulance Squad came first. When they saw who was attached to the turtle, the East Hampton PD weren't far behind. The Appendage's husband was released of his appendage and treated for a turtle bite at Southampton Hospital. Then he was given his own private cell at East Hampton Police Headquarters in Wainscott. Police found a bloody filet knife in his truck. It wasn't fish guts stuck to it, that's for sure. Some guys can't part with their gear, no matter what. Guess he figured it was still a good knife.

As for Grunt, when the medical examiner was through with him, his body was sewn up like the Frankenstein monster and he was taken to Yardley Pino Funeral Home on 27. His ex-wife paid for the expenses. Someone overheard her saying he should be used for bait in the upcoming shark tournament. His buddies found that cold. But they never lived with him.

It was a small wake. Grunt never had kids. His mother, the prostitute, was long dead. He didn't make a lot of friends in his life. It was an eclectic group of mourners. His whore boat partners, Dragger, Ass and Em were there. A bunch of Sportys showed up, whether out of allegiance to one of their own, morbid curiosity, or to gloat, no one really knew. The rest were women. Hookers of another sort. The girls he frequented at the escort service in the city before he starting catching Mermaids.

Speaking of Mermaids, only one showed up. Saffron. She cried like a baby. Touching. The Appendage sat in the back row, doped up on Valium. She wore a tight green dress with a kelly green shawl draped over her head. A silver pendant dipped into her cleavage. Dragger did a double take. A large rhinestone turtle hung between her breasts. Grunt would have appreciated that detail.

Chase was there. Not by choice, but for appearance sake. Em didn't want undue attention drawn to the whore boat. The casket was closed, a glossy framed 8x10 of Grunt sat on top. Grunt at the Montauk Marine Basin, standing next to his prize shark, the one that won him the tournament that year. He was shirtless and brown as a berry, grinning like a fool and those steely eyes of his hidden behind his Maui Jims. He had one hand on the fish and the other on the filet knife in his belt.

The bloodstains on his khaki shorts were fresh. Dragger couldn't help but think how the Appendage's husband scored one for the sharks yesterday.

Grunt was cremated. His ashes scattered over the Canyons during the upcoming shark tournament. Sporty's final resting place in the belly of the creatures he hunted. Poetic justice you could say.

Chapter Thirty-Two

Em neglected to mention one small point about their new whore boat captain. He wasn't all there. Elevator didn't reach the top floor. Could be the booze. At times though, the Admiral was completely lucid. Others times, not so much. Perhaps he was so brilliant, he snapped. Too much information in one man's brain. He knew history that was a fact. He could rattle off dates of wars and battles with a good buzz on. He loved to preach. Specifically, he loved to bless people. They say he used to be a priest. Maybe that explained it. The Admiral wasn't talking, even though he was always talking.

He would space right out in the middle of a conversation, or what emulated one. You were lost and he was off on a tangent, hands waving as if he still had the incense burner on a chain, smoking out the congregation. Then he would suddenly leave his barstool and go to the other end of the room to engage a perfect stranger, if the spirit moved him. And apparently it did.

People said he was fervently passionate. Others called him an old souse. Everyone agreed he was a motor mouth. He was like the crawl at the bottom of the television on the news channel. Going twenty four seven. This behavior could be tolerated in a bar, no problem, where let's face it, no one really cares about proper decorum. Em and her partner's concern was keeping him in one place, the boat. Mostly in the wheelhouse.

The Admiral was always on. Like a

leprechaun, he jumped around Liars, dancing to the jukebox and telling anyone within earshot, how he knew the singer way back when or how the song came to be written. Then he blessed the jukebox and yourself if you sang along. He looked like the Travelocity gnome come to life and run through the not so gentle cycle, minus the sweet smelling soap powder. And what exactly were those bits stuck in his beard? Pieces of insulation?

Yet there was an unnamable aura about him. His eyes were a holy blue, like the picture of Jesus on your mother's kitchen wall. Was he a messenger in a paint splattered jacket and Mr. Bojangles pants, sent here to save us? Or just a raving alcoholic who stayed too long at the fair? It didn't matter. A better sea captain, you would not find.

Em knew him best. She was the one stuck behind the bar listening to him all those years. She swore he wouldn't hurt a fly. Her partners believed her. Dragger said it was all rosy until he decided to preach to a boatful of Mermaids or had a whim to baptize himself in the middle of the ocean. But they needed him. Admiral Joey Flapjaws would be the savior of the whore boat. Or its crucifier. Time would tell.

Chapter Thirty-Three

The air in Liars was so thick you could cut it with a knife. The laws that governed the rest of the population did not apply. "Smoke 'em if you got 'em," ruled. Dragger smoked his head off plenty there. That's what the little plastic cups filled with water on the bar were for, since the orange melmac ashtrays disappeared. Cups full of butt juice. I wonder if anyone ever drank one by mistake.

Liars was the one place where you could count on things remaining the same. "If it ain't broke, don't fix it." The owner lived by those words. Liars belonged to the fishermen. And the locals, who relied on their home away from home. Every summer there was a new trendy bar popping up on the scene. Liars was unaffected. No one cared what you wore or who you were. If you thought differently, you were in the wrong bar. Drink, talk about fishing, and listen to the jukebox, that was enough. And so it went. Until the karaoke crowd arrived.

"Are you fucking kidding me?" That was the general reaction when the guy walked in with his equipment. "This ain't no karaoke bar, man." Hostile looks and unease hung in the smoky air. Luckily the dude was local. Not Montauk, but close enough. Still, you have to grow on people. You can't insinuate yourself into a tradition.

The scenery changed some. New faces appeared at the bar every week. Besides the regulars, always male dominated, there were women who were more familiar with a nail file than

133

a filet knife. Just regular people who wanted to toss back a few cocktails and sing a few songs on a Friday night after putting in a full week of whatever they did to make the rent. The owner's girlfriend, CC, had a serious set of pipes. The fishermen were always up to listen to her belt out Oh Darling or At Last. The owner, Vinny, was her biggest fan. Some of the other singers weren't half bad. On a good night, it could be downright entertaining. If you didn't want to partake in the songfest, you ignored them and went about your drinking and talking.

The DJ had a problem with the smoking. He made regular announcements to "Take your cigarettes outside, it's a beautiful night." He was a pain in the ass, but they respected the guy, most of the time. It couldn't have been easy being trapped back there, without a window, listening to the same goddamn songs week after week.

He always let Dragger sing War Pigs, when he was around. Since he gave up Jack, he didn't hang out at Liars so much. That and the frequent times he threw someone threw the window. You got banned for fighting. You had to earn your way back into the owner's good graces. And the bartender's. It was funny to watch the tourist's reaction to Dragger's rendition of Black Sabbath. Here they thought they were going to some quaint little fishermen's shack when suddenly they had entered the third ring of hell. Dragger owned that song. If you expected The Carpenters or Frank Sinatra, I'd say you would be disappointed, but that wasn't true. You heard it all there. The mood could change on a dime.

Right after you wanted to kill yourself when someone sang a suicide song, a group would get up and do Crosby Stills and Nash like they meant it. Johnny, Lord of the Manor, doing Satisfaction. A guy called JB, nailing REM or White Wedding. That one used to be Bobby Buca's song. He's drinking his Sambuca in heaven now. The thing is, there weren't really any divas. No American Idol wannabes. Liars wouldn't be Liars if that happened. Occasionally though, in the summer, they had this karaoke contest. The atmosphere changed. The divas came out of the woodwork like carpenter ants. Even the karaoke crack whores didn't like it. Where were these people all year? It was easy to understand how the fishermen felt when they thought their bar was being invaded by karaoke.

Dragger was meeting the Admiral Joey Flapjaws at Liars for a chat of sorts. Probably not the best place to discuss business, but Dragger had to see for himself if Em's idea to hire the Admiral held water. The problem was it happened to be Friday and the karaoke crowd was in the house. The Admiral kept flying off his barstool to groove to the next song and bless the singer. He liked Janis Joplin's incarnation, a woman named Helen, doing her rendition of Piece Of My Heart. She got a double blessing from Admiral Flapjaws.

Some guy named Harryoke, with a full beard, is doing his Tevyeh imitation of If I Were A Rich Man. Dragger is thinking "Are you for fucking real, man?" The Admiral is off again and soon the two of them, Harryoke and the Admiral, are leaping and tiptoeing their way around the bar, "deedledeeing" all the way. In the meantime Clint the lobsterman is yelling "Play some Doors, motherfucker," at the top of his lungs. You can't make this shit up.

Next thing, the Admiral takes a shine to a little woman his own size and all he wants to do is dance with her. I think the woman was a little frightened, but she was a good sport. He called her St. Ann for no reason anybody could figure out, including the woman, whose name was J Diddy. It's Montauk, nobody has regular names.

The Whistler's husband is called Pot Roast. His brother, Cornbread. Dragger said the two went together. I didn't quite get that, but who argued with Dragger? There was Ginny Ray, hard G, hard living fisherman, Tommy Two Shoes, Johnny Flat Top, Johnny Fresh Squeeze, Brandino, Shady, the Gatekeeper, the Transformer, TJ. TK, Chris I, Chris II, Chris C., Smokin' Joe, Cowboy, Country Dianne, Country Colleen & Honey, Fisherman Rich, Big Rich, Buddy Love, Sal the Package, Peebo, Dancing Carl, the Diva, the Matts, and the Goddesses. And that's just a couple dozen.

When Dragger finally got the Admiral's attention and a free blessing, they shook hands on the deal. The Admiral was officially their new whore boat captain. He informed Dragger that "It would be an honor to serve her majesty and the needs of all good men." Dragger only hoped he was referring to Em and didn't think he was joining the Queen's Royal Navy. It was a gamble going with the Admiral, but they had little choice and a floating brothel to keep afloat. Dragger said good night and the Admiral went in search of St. Ann for another dance.

Chapter Thirty-Four

If anyone could sober up the Admiral it was Ass. Not that Ass was a teetotaler. He liked a cold one every now and again. But the guy drank an inordinate amount of tea. Earl Grey being his top choice, followed by English Breakfast, Darjeeling, and some vile tasting green tea he brewed loose. So they let him at it. The Admiral ate it up. Thought he was being called to high tea by Earl Sputenridge, whom he insisted on calling Ass. Dragger didn't care if he called him the Pillsbury Doughboy, as long as he got sober enough to captain the whore boat.

The Admiral adored Chase. "Well who wouldn't?" Dragger said with a tinge of jealousy. Chase at this stage had given up her Mermaid aspirations and Ass had a smile on his face every morning. She still had her heart set on working aboard the Lily Virginia in some capacity, so Em made her the whore boat's official masseuse. Chase had her physical therapy credentials, so it was perfect. The Mermaids loved her and they were her chief clientele. Her only clientele, besides Ass, Em, Dragger and now the Admiral. The johns were off limits. Ass wasn't borrowing trouble and Dragger wasn't one hundred percent sure it was Ass who pulled the trigger on Grunt.

Chase had a cousin who liked to hunt game upstate. He taught her to shoot a gun when she was a kid. The girl knew how to aim and make it count, that's all I'm saying. And who knows what being raped does to the psyche? They didn't need any dead johns to contend with. Dragger had no intention of becoming the next Sweeney Todd.

Chapter Thirty-Five

"I love your name," she said to Chase. What was this Mermaid's name again? Amber? No. Pearl. No. A stone of some sort. Garnet, that was it.

"Thank you. It means dweller at the hunting ground," Chase said, putting a little more pressure on Garnet's lower back.

"Interesting. Ouch, that's a bit sore, hon. I had some real big johns this week. They like me to ride them backwards. It's a bitch on the back."

Chase eased up. "Sorry. You should try yoga. It releases the low back. I could show you some poses if you want."

"Darlin,' all I do is pose six days a week. But I appreciate the advice. Hey you ever think about my line of work yourself? You got a killer mouth and a bedtime body if you don't mind me saying. Bet you're awesome naked."

"I don't know about awesome, I get by. Actually, my mother was a stripper. I kind of got turned off by the whole entertaining men thing. I'm too moody anyway. Men like compliance. I don't take orders well."

"Men like women, period, darlin'. Mostly as long as you're breathing and smell good and can take the one-eyed wonder worm and pretend it's the best lollypop in town, you're golden. Simple creatures, the opposite sex. Trust me."

Chase laughed. Garnet picked her head up and looked back at Chase. "You do like cock, sugar, don't you? Or did I read you all wrong? I slept with a woman once. She had the hairiest bush this side of the Erie Canal. I taught her what a Brazilian was. She taught me how to use my tongue to its best advantage. I owe her a debt if I ever see her again. So your old lady stripped? Any good? Christ, my jaw is killing me."

"My mother was an amateur. And I like men, by the way. Garnet, may I suggest you lay off the oral for awhile. Is that possible? You might have a case of TMJ." Chase wasn't being facetious. Garnet was known for her oral expertise. Chase kept her ears open. She knew each Mermaid's specialty.

Garnet cracked up. "TM what? Give up the oral? You're not serious? Anyway, let me know if you're ever interested. I wouldn't charge you. My pleasure. Betcha you wax?"

"I do as a matter of fact. I'm honored, but Aspen is keeping me in cunnilingus heaven, thanks."

"Hah. Good for you, sugar. Lucky boy, that Aspen. Ah… that's it, you got the spot… You got special hands, anyone tell you that? Yeah, go deep, darlin,' make me moan like a two dollar whore at fleet week."

"Christ, Garnet, anyone listening would think we were getting it on. But okay, you asked for it." Chase rubbed some warm oil on her hands and found the right spot on Garnet's back. The star Mermaid let out a moan to wake the dead.

Saffron was Chase's next client. She was the youngest Mermaid on the Lily Virginia. Innocence had nothing to do with youth in her case. Her disposition was as hard as her perfect little butt.

Raised by a pothead hippie mother up around Big Sur, no father in the picture, Saffron ran away from home at 15. She ended up on the proverbial Greyhound, New York City bound and wound up working for an escort service.

Her absentee father was a doctor in India where Saffron's mother lived for a time on her trust fund. Saffron never met him but she inherited his exotic coloring and gorgeous dark almond shaped eyes. Her free spirited nature was her mother's contribution. Saffron had no fears and no filter. She spoke her mind no matter what was on it. For kicks, she broke up marriages because she could. The God given gift of her body and face and her willingness to do anything sexually, for a price, she left more than a few men begging for more. Their groveling in particular turned her on and the lucky fella got the prize of primo sex that he never experienced with his suburban PTA wife who couldn't give a proper blowjob if her life depended on it.

Saffron could make even the less endowed seem like they were King Kong. She was that good an actress. Academy Award material. She got one john to buy her boobs and another an apartment on the Upper East Side. She had no girlfriends because she didn't like girls. They were nosy and catty and jealous. And they didn't like her either. She might take their boyfriends; they weren't stupid. Neither was Saffron. She probably already had and they were the last to know about it. Guys couldn't refuse her. It wasn't her fault if she was irresistible.

Grunt brought her on the whore boat via his friend who owned the escort service. She wanted a change from the city for a while. And she could make more money on the boat. To her it was a game. And she would win it. When she had what she deemed enough money, she was taking that long awaited trip to India to find her father and give him a piece of her mind. Or maybe she would seduce him first and then tell him who she was.

Chase did not hit it off with her at all. But Saffron was just a kid really and Chase was always a professional. Chase didn't care for Saffron's attitude and how she thought she was God's gift to men. She also liked Aspen and Chase knew it.

" Hi. I so need a good massage, Chase. I am so tired." Saffron was stark naked when she answered her door. Chase walked into her room. "Hello, Saffron. Maybe you should take your Flintstones vitamins, sweetie. Or take an extra day off."

"Very funny. I did thirty guys this week and the week isn't over. I need a vacation. But I need the money more so give me a good massage will you? Make me all brand new. Make me a princess with a nice tight…"

"Hey, knock it off. I'm not your fairy godmother. Stop complaining or go back to school. You have choices. Have some respect for yourself. And me."

"You're not my mother."

"Thank heaven for small favors. Lucky for you, or I'd kick your little ass, now lie down on your back and cover up your stuff. I didn't come here for a show."

Saffron sulked for a second or two and did as she was told. Chase knew she was secretly craving discipline, which she'd never had. Saffron confused her sassy independence with self-confidence and freedom. But she was on her back for a living when she had the brains to go to medical school. It gave Chase a headache but she wasn't working on a whore boat to save the world. Still it bugged the hell out of her.

"Hey, Chase, is Aspen hung? Because I could tell you some terrific positions to make it feel really good for you. Grunt was huge. I miss him. He used to spank me, over his knee and then I would…"

"Saffron, shhh… close your eyes and listen to the waves. Here's the lavender eye pillow. No talking, sweetie. Good girl." Chase covered Saffron's eyes and turned on the white noise machine and dimmed the lights. The baby hooker was quiet for the rest of the session.

Chapter Thirty-Six

Chase checked her Mermaid schedule. She had two massages later that afternoon. Heaven and Lyric. Heaven had neck issues. Lyric just needed what she called a tune up. Chase knew Lyric appreciated the simple pleasure of somebody touching her without wanting sex in any shape or form. No happy ending. No talk of clients. Just her own happiness for a change. It was a healthy attitude. Chase looked forward to their easy talks. But right now Chase was on her way to the Admiral's cabin. Dragger had switched cabins with Grunt's old one. Chase would not have to revisit that horrible day with Grunt. She knocked on the Admiral's door.

"Why if it isn't Maybelle Hooker. Come on in."

"Admiral? I'm Chase, remember? Maybelle was my grandmother."

"I know that. Just having some fun with you. I remember Maybelle quite well. I have one of her rugs in my house. She was a talented lady. Very affectionate too, if I recall…"

"You're a card, Admiral. Are you ready for your massage?"

"Was Custer ready for his last stand? Do your worst, Chase. And relax, I'm not as crazy as they think. We'll become fast friends, you'll see. Strangers are friends you haven't yet met."

"That's a nice thought. Now have you been using the castor oil packs like I suggested?"

"Oh indeed. And my back is nearly singing

with excitement. I might be ready for a Mermaid to swim my way tonight. Bless those dear girls." He laughed and there was a distinct twinkle in his eye, his gnomish face aglow.

"Well, that's progress. Now if you would lie on your belly, I'll work on your back. So, is there a favorite Mermaid?"

"I like when Heaven comes to me. How can you not love a gal named Heaven? The others are fine, and I don't begrudge them their specialties, it's all wonderful. I don't judge anyone. There are always people greater and less than us."

"You're full of witticisms, Admiral."

"Some people think I'm just full of it," he laughed. "Don't regret not becoming a Mermaid yourself, Maybelle's granddaughter. Take it from me, regrets are a waste of time. Besides, you and the Earl will have a far better time of it. You have to have faith."

"I appreciate that, Admiral. Aspen is a keeper for sure."

The Admiral chuckled and turned back at her and winked.

After his massage the Admiral wanted Chase to have tea with him. She couldn't refuse him and she enjoyed their little chats. "Will the Earl be joining us?"

"No, Admiral, he's busy at the moment. Boat stuff with Dragger."

"Gotcha. Did I tell you my father was a patriot? In Dublin. The truth. He was at the General Post Office when they shot all those men. He was one of them. It was 1916 and they were fighting for Ireland's freedom from the British. No offence to the Earl, now, Chase."

"None taken. Aspen's mother was Irish."

"Bless the Earl. Anyway, terrible times. It was the Easter Rising. Not Jesus, no. The rising up of Irish men to be free. Started on the Monday and lasted five days. Patrick Pearse was the leader for the Nationalists. He led the Rising. They executed him along with others. Eamon deValera was there. He was the other leader. He escaped the firing squad. His father was an American you see. The British didn't want that on their heads.

He went on to lead Sinn Fein. Controversy surrounded him. Some liked his politics, others didn't care for them. Yeats wrote about the Rising. Brilliant man, Yeats. Let me see if I remember the words…

"We know their dream; enough
To know they dreamed and are dead;
And what if excess of love
Bewildered them till they died?
I write it out in a verse—
MacDonagh and MacBride
And Connolly and Pearse
Now and in time to be,
Wherever green is worn,
Are changed. Changed utterly:
A terrible beauty is born."

"That's beautiful, Admiral. And very sad. I'm sorry about your father."

"Sorry doesn't change history. But I thank you. Blood will always be shed for freedom. Until we find another way. I'm too old, I leave that to the young. Never let them take your freedom, Chase.

Your god-given right. These words are not wasted on you I imagine…"

"No sir, Admiral. 'Freedom's just another word for nothing left to lose…"

"Well said. Janis Joplin recorded in 1970, months before her death. Written by Kris Kristofferson. Originally sung by Roger Miller."

"How do you know all those facts?"

"My mind is like one of those bingo cages with all the numbers rolling around. In my case, it's trivia and history. And I've always been an avid music lover. An aficionado, if you will."

"Admiral, I have enjoyed our chat. Thank you."

"Your most welcome, Maybelle's granddaughter."

Chase gave him a hug and went on her way.

Chapter Thirty-Seven

Dragger had more than a few pet peeves, but the one that really got under his skin was someone leaving a cryptic message on his voice mail. Especially if that crypt keeper was his ex-wife. They lived in the same town and shared a daughter and that was the end of it. Lake minded her business where Dragger was concerned and he did the same. So why was she suddenly calling him? Lake prefaced her mystery message with "This has nothing to do with Tribeca. But it's important." There was no reason for the phone call in Dragger's mind. They didn't do small talk. In fact they didn't talk, period. If he saw her in town, he nodded. She might wave from her car or push her hair behind her ears. It was a nervous habit that she knew bugged the hell out of him.

Lake knew about the whore boat, he was sure of it. She would keep her opinion and judgment to herself. She did not tell Tribeca about it, adult or not. Not for Dragger's benefit. She didn't tell her because that required talking about Dragger, something she never did. When that door closed, it stayed closed. So why the urgent contact now? Dragger punched in her number, which was not in his phone but etched in his brain, and waited.

"This is Lake, please leave me a message and have a peaceful day." Cheery voice mail. Another pet peeve. "It's Dragger. What's up? And I was having a peaceful day, until you called." He clicked off the phone. He was hungry and not in the mood for leftovers. He threw on a jacket and headed for Gaviola's. A nice roast beef on a roll with horseradish and mustard was calling his name.

His belly full, Dragger swung by the village and Lake's store, Peaceful Pieces.

Lake was alone inside the shop; Dragger could see her sorting jewelry through the window. He stubbed out his cigarette and opened the door. Lake looked up. There was no smile and no hair tucking either. Just that icy stare she was so good at delivering. "Dragger."

"Lake." Two can play this game, he thought.

"You obviously got my message, or were you in the market for a peace sign? Maybe some earrings? Do Mermaids wear earrings?"

Dragger's lunch was repeating on him. He reached into his pocket for his Tums.

"So this your way of opening the lines of communication? Or did you suddenly miss me? I know, you want a job on the boat. You still got it, by the way. Age has been kind to you, Lake. You know what they say, you can't take it with you."

"None of the above. And I have no interest in becoming a Mermaid. This is serious." She walked over to the door and put the closed sign facing out. She came back and stood behind the counter. "Look, I am just the messenger. But don't make the mistake of taking this lightly. This group has no tolerance for your boat business. They aim to stop it."

"Hang on, let me get this straight, my boat business? What goddamn business is it of...which group is this? The holy roller hags? The bible bitches? Who? And why now? This ain't new,

Lake. And it's not happening in town, so what's the problem. Who exactly has the nosy bug up their ass?"

"Don't raise your voice to me, Dragger. I'll throw you the hell out of here, I don't need this." She tucked an unruly blonde tendril behind her ear. "I wanted you to hear it from me. For Tribeca's sake."

"Tribeca is a grown woman."

"Who thinks her father runs a party boat."

"Some might call it that."

"Don't get cute. You know what I mean."

"Did you just compliment me?"

"No. Now will you listen to me or not?"

"I'm all ears, Lake."

"You're all balls."

"Thank you. Two compliments. This must be my lucky day."

"You've heard of the Montauk Morality Mission?"

Dragger laughed. "You're joking, right? Is this the 1800's and the Temperance Movement, Sister Sharon?"

"Very funny. Let me finish. There is an organization in town that is against what the bars and dress codes and loose morals of its citizens have become. People have been affected and they are taking a stand. They believe it is time for a shift. They meet every…"

"Don't tell me, Monday?"

Lake shook her head. "I am trying to be serious. You do not want to mess with these people. They want the whore boat stopped. They are against making a profit from sex. It is giving the town a bad name."

"Are they against sex for free? Apparently not, because that's been going on since Eve, so what are you really on about? Sounds to me like the moral Q tips are whining about nothing. Do they want a senior discount? Our Mermaids like 'em old and young and in between. We just need a disclaimer if they have a pacemaker."

"Go ahead and joke. When you get shut down by the county and they drag your name and our daughter's through the mud, then will you be happy?"

"Happy is a relative term. You should know that, you're a Buddhist. Who exactly is heading up this terror squad? Are they packing weapons? Gonna beat me with their walkers or pummel me with mothballs? Stop wasting my time. Tell the truth, you missed yourself some Dragger…"

Hair tuck. "The names are confidential. It was a courtesy to me to let you know before they contact the authorities. I thought you might, just maybe, appreciate that, but who was I kidding?"

"Don't get all dramatic on me, Lake. And the authorities are our clients. Nobody is shutting us down, relax."

"Don't tell me to relax." Lake's pet peeve. He forgot. That's a lie.

"Why don't you tell the M&M's is it? They don't have to get their Depends in a twist. We take people out fishing and what they do way out in the middle of the ocean is their own business. What happened, did they get tired of fighting the Smurf Lodge? Isn't there a rare bird they can fight to save and leave my Mermaids alone?"

"Let's just say there is something bigger at stake here. Excuse me, *your* Mermaids?"

"Did I miss a step? Haven't we been divorced for more years than I can remember? Are you jealous, Lake? Where's your little surfer boy? Did he find a little surfer girl?"

"Fuck you, Dragger." Bingo. "Sky and I are just fine, thanks for asking. Anyway, I thought you were the captain, not the pimp." Score one for the ex-knife.

"Glad to see you haven't lost your sense of humor…or your edge. Now can we stop this verbal ping pong and get to the nitty gritty? I have people waiting for me."

"Who? Some Mermaid with her legs up in the air?" Dragger whistled. "Whoa, you are in a bad way, Lake. Just how long ago did Sky boy fly the coop? The anger is very sexy by the way."

"Fuck you."

"That an invitation? I can put off my meeting for an hour…"

" Stay here, I have some papers you might be interested in seeing." Lake walked to the back of the store and closed a door behind her. Dragger followed her.

"I told you to wait up front."

"You also told me fuck you. I thought I would oblige."

"I am trying to help you, Dragger."

"Likewise."

"This can't happen. Just take the papers. Read over them and get back to me. I'll tell the group you need some time."

"And you would do this for me, because…"

"Because of Tribeca."

"Right. So why are you excited right now?"

"What?" Lake crossed her arms in front of her chest. "Go away, Dragger."

"Say it more convincingly, and I will."

"Dragger…"

"Yes?"

"Close the door."

Chapter Thirty-Eight

There are certain times when alcohol is necessary. Medicinal. This was one of those times. But for Dragger, one shot of the devil and he would be on a bender there was no coming back from, so coffee and chocolate were going to have to suffice. He opened a Cadbury Fruit and Nut and turned another page of the manifesto Lake gave him.

So Heaven was apparently not heaven sent after all. Well, she was, that was her name, Heaven Sent. But their very popular, very pleasing Mermaid was hiding out on a whore boat, biding her time, until she got her orders to blow up the next government building? A terrorist with tits. Just what he needed.

The paperwork on her was incredible. She had posed as a teacher, a nurse, a nun, a ballet dancer and a yoga instructor. She never married. No children. Grunt met her at the escort service in the city, her last gig before she joined the Mermaids. How did Lake get this information? Dragger bet it had little to do with the Montauk Morality Mission and more to do with someone who knew both Dragger and Lake. Dragger crunched a hazelnut and thought about that. They had a snooper aboard the whore boat. Was it Lake? No, she was just the messenger. Buddhists generally don't work as spies. It wasn't Ass or Em, Dragger knew that. Definitely not the Admiral. That left Chase. She had access to the Mermaid quarters. Did Heaven know anything was missing or did Chase make copies? While the Admiral had his visit from Heaven tonight, Dragger would do a little snooping of his own.

Heaven blew up casinos. That was her MO. Her next target was Foxwoods and Mohegan Sun, across the water in Connecticut. She already had her assignment as a dealer. Why wasn't she caught before? Dragger almost choked on his nut bar. Heaven was actually Herbert before she started her rage against the machines. Heaven, on paper, did not exist. Herbert Sent was a school teacher in Mississippi who joined a Mennonite homestead and wouldn't harm a fly if it landed on his shoofly pie. The day Heaven decided to come out, as it were, Herbert literally lost his balls.

Why casinos? Dragger read on. Herbert/Heaven's father was a gambling man. Down in New Orleans. His mother, however, was not a tailor. Anyway, Daddy Sent, loved the blackjack tables. And the women who brought him whiskey and stayed the night. So for Mama Sent and her little son, Herbert, money was scarce. When daddy was around, he wasn't very generous or very nice. And he couldn't bear a mama's boy, which Herbert was, right down to his penchant for trying on mama's nightgowns and shoes. Daddy Sent was mortified. "That boy needs to join the army, mother," he told Mama Sent. And when he turned eighteen that is just what Herbert did. Private Sent was an exemplary soldier. And when he came home, he found a nice calling as a teacher in Mississippi, far enough away from his Daddy. Mama Sent had since passed on and after he visited her grave and paid his respects with a café au lait and beignet, one for himself and one for Mama, he repacked and jumped on a Greyhound.

What ever happened between the teaching gig and Mennonite homestead and now, only Heaven knows. Dragger couldn't very well ask her, she might decide to blow up the whore boat. You never know what sets people off. Or what they have going on inside their psyches or psychosis as it were. Heaven could have fooled Dragger and he was nobody's fool. She just didn't look like a terrorist. She didn't have those I don't get much sleep crazy eyes or behave in any strange manner, besides her casino bomb habit. If you put Heaven in a light blue robe, she would look like the Virgin Mary heading for Bethlehem. Angelic. Something besides the genitalia went radically wrong.

Heaven set her bombs to detonate when there were few people around. She wasn't looking for collateral damage, she just wanted to level the casinos. More like she was punishing the establishments that drew her father in, not the gamblers themselves.

This time she wasn't going to punish anyone because Dragger was going to stop her.

It was a shame they would lose her as a Mermaid, she was a favorite, a top earner. But as her father would say, you win some, you lose some.

Dragger thought about Grunt and how he raved about Heaven when he recruited her from the escort service. It gave Dragger a little burst of pleasure knowing that Grunt was bragging about sleeping with a man. Even if Grunt didn't know Heaven was Herbert once upon a time, Grunt was homophobic and that would have set him off completely. Dragger scratched his head. Come to think of it, Grunt like to brag, period. What if he did a little pillow talking to Heaven about the new Mermaid he just scored? And maybe Heaven would like a threesome with himself and Chase for instance? Heaven liked Chase. In a protective sister kind of way. Heaven didn't share. What if Heaven heard that Grunt raped Chase? Would she want revenge for her friend? Was it a far stretch from blowing up a casino to gutting a rapist? Maybe the Appendage's husband didn't slice up Grunt for sushi after all.

Chapter Thirty-Nine

Dragger found Heaven's black book. In the world of Mermaids, that was equivalent to finding the black box. All her johns and their visits were recorded. Next to that, their preferences, fetishes, etc. Heaven included her own critiques. She had favorites. One of them was River Denero. Detective River Denero. Dragger's old buddy. River could be trusted. He was retired from the Chicago Police Department and came out to Montauk to fish. Dragger took him out plenty. River bought himself a little ramshackle fisherman's cottage down on West Lake Drive and a small boat. He minded his own business. Dragger drank with him in the beginning, when Dragger drank. Lately, if he ran into River, Dragger was sucking down a coffee. River had stories, but he wasn't a bullshit artist. Dragger appreciated that. River was a straight up kind of guy. If you needed a favor, he was your man.

Dragger had to wonder how much River knew about Heaven. If he had to guess, it was nothing except she was good at her job. Time to find out. Dragger punched in River's number on his cell and waited. "Hello…"

"River, hey man, Dragger here. I need to talk to you. You busy?"

"Nope. Too windy out there for fishing, so I'm all yours."

"Meet me at my place in an hour?"

"You got it, Dragger."

Dragger waved River inside from the

161

kitchen window. "Nice view, man. I haven't been up here in ages." Dragger offered him a coffee. "Black, right?"

"Yep. Good memory. So what's cooking? Mermaid trouble? Sorry about Grunt. Poor fucker. Somebody had it in for him."

"Yeah, poor Grunt. Shame. But you hit the nail on the head. I got a Mermaid problem. Heaven."

"No way. What could she have done? Or did someone get rough? You let me know who it is and I'll take care of him."

"It's not like that. Heaven herself is the problem. Sit down. Let me fill you in…"

Dragger was just about finished with the story of Heaven when River interrupted him.

"You know who her uncle was, right?"

"Jack the Ripper?"

River smiled. "Skinny D'Amato."

"And he would be?"

"The Father of Atlantic City. Owner of the 500 Club. Friend of the Rat Pack. His place was a big Mafioso hangout in the 40's. Daddy Sent was there, I'm sure of it. Mama Sent probably worked a few shifts, if you catch my drift… she was quite a looker. I've seen pictures. Daddy Sent is deceased. Gout. Diabetes. Liver Failure. The Trifecta. Drink did him in. Who would ever believe Heaven was once a guy? She's every inch a woman. No pun intended."

"That part I'm not concerned about, River. The casino bombing, I am. How do we stop her without calling the FBI and turning this whole thing into a media feeding frenzy? I got a business to run, man."

"Leave it to me. You say she did this before?"

"Tried. It was a dud. No one was hurt. Somewhere in Nevada. Outside of Vegas."

"So she's not exactly on a Wanted poster?"

"Not yet."

"Where did you get this information?"

"Lake. But I think I know how that happened."

"Snoop on the boat?"

Dragger wondered how he knew that. Then he remembered River was a cop. "Yep."

"I'll get her off the boat, Dragger, no worries. I like her a lot. We can go down to the Keys. She can't be a Mermaid forever. I know a woman shrink from the job. She'll get Heaven to talk about her Daddy and maybe give her some meds. A little R&R down south. Heaven will be fine."

Dragger rubbed his beard stubble. "You must really like her, man. This is a big responsibility. You sure about this?"

"Yep. Get rid of any manifesto you have and anything else that suggests her plans. I'll talk to her and explain how she can come with me or have her face and history all over the newspapers. I know what choice she'll make."

"Okay. I knew I was right to call you. One thing that's eating at me though… do you think Heaven is capable of close range violence?"

"Spit it out, Dragger. You're talking about Grunt? No way she gutted him like that. She was kind of fond of him. I never understood that affection, but the girl's a Mermaid, right? They have to like all men, more or less."

"Yeah, it was just a fleeting thought."

"Let it go. I'll get her out of town. No worries for the boat. Or the casinos."

"Great. Thanks, River. I owe you one."

"You're giving me Heaven. Believe me that is worth more than you know. Or maybe you do know?"

"Nope. Haven't had the pleasure. I'm still trying to figure out why I boned my ex yesterday."

"Lake? Really? Good for you. I'd say that was inevitable. Talk about sexual tension...."

"Pent-up ain't the word for it. The woman is an animal."

"Lucky you. But did you check and see if your balls are still there?" River laughed.

"Present and accounted for, just on the sore side. I had no idea Buddhists practiced oral sex so fervently."

River laughed. "Lucky you. Hey, don't worry about Heaven."

"I'm more worried about hell these days."

River left and Dragger took the Manifesto Lake gave him and threw it in the bathtub and lit the edges with his lighter. He washed the ashes down the drain.

Chapter Forty

My name is Emory Ann Talkhouse and I've lived in Montauk my entire life. My ancestors, The Montaukett Indians, founded this place known as The End. Before cattle ranches, railroads, oceanfront motels and fishing tournaments were a dream in men's minds, my people were dug in here. Their remains are buried on this piece of heaven known as Montauk, their "island home." Ruins of Montaukett gathering places are evident all over Montauk, particularly in places like Big Reed. Deep in the woods I would go on long walks with my Grandmother and listen to her tales of the Makiaweesug, the fairies or little people that lived in the woods. Grandmother taught me about strength and the power of believing in the unbelievable. I understood from a young age that I didn't need proof of all the universe's wonders. Grandmother explained to me how there were no Montaukett women chiefs, but that could change someday. "You alone are in charge of your destiny, Emory," she told me that day as we gazed out at Big Reed Pond. "Never give away your power."

Madam of a whore boat is not quite what Grandmother had in mind for me, but I run my own ship and that is what counts. I keep a little Montaukett magic up my sleeve to have handy when I need it. For instance in the case of Grunt. No, I didn't murder him. I merely suggested to The Appendage's husband that he might want to go down to Liars and see what his wife was up to that night. The rest he took upon himself. Some people have a rage inside that unleashes a hideous darkness capable of unspeakable violence. Jealousy isn't called the green-eyed monster for nothing.

Heaven I couldn't have foreseen. That Mermaid had her stuff together. She pleased her clients, kept her quarters clean and brought in a steady flow of cash. River was a love to take care of Heaven for us. Now there was a man I wouldn't kick out of the bed for eating saltines. The thing sticking in my craw the most was that Montauk Morality Mission nonsense. Were these people joking? I could tell you stories that would curl your hair about some of them. Hell, all of them. Now suddenly they were holier than thou? Give me a break.

Shannie, the leader, was a porcupine if there ever was one. If she had as many sticking out as sticking in. Maybe she was irked because the Mermaids got paid and she gave it away. I'd offer her a job, but then I'd have to listen to her jabber jaws going twenty four/seven. She would wind up going overboard by the end of the day. No, I would remind her of all the kissing and telling she'd done at Liars, while she dragged hard on her Marlboro Lights and said "Pour me another one, Em, will you?" I knew too much and Shannie was about to have a replay from yours truly. She might have her little group fooled, but not for long.

Cal was another one. Mr. Clean as a whistle. Right. The amount of powder that went up that man's nose would choke an elephant. Who the hell was he to tell us the whore boat was immoral? A guy who screwed his brother's fiancé before getting him blind drunk at the bachelor party. Ditto at the wedding. "One more shot, bro, be a fucking man..." Poor bastard was useless on his wedding night. Passed out cold. Cal screwed the bride in the next room. Three times before morning. His brother never found out. Cal however got a case of loose lips on his favorite barstool at Liars. "Em I got a confession to make. Hit me again. I gotta tell you something..."

Get ready, Cal. I am so ready to take my punch.

When I heard the whore bride, "Jammin' Pam," was against the whore boat, I almost choked on my Cornflakes. Her habit of sleeping with her brother in law didn't stop after the wedding. She and Cal were probably still jammin' while her husband stayed naïve as the day is long. I'd say he deserved what he got for having his head in the clouds, but a nicer guy you wouldn't meet. Heartless bitches always seem to find a sucker. I would take great pleasure in informing Mrs. Revolving Pussy, though she had a short memory, I didn't.

Those were the key players, and I had the goods on every last one of them. Their Montauk Morality Mission was about to become Montauk mincemeat. The whore boat was here to stay. Just I case I run into any snags, a walk in Big Reed couldn't hurt. A little conjuring up of the Makiaweesug for a bit of help was in order. It was a gorgeous day and I know every path and hidden turn in those woods like the back of my hand. I headed for East Lake Drive. One quick stop at Susan's market for some sage and a coffee and I was on the trail.

Chapter Forty-One

Em should have listened to Susan. She urged her to stay awhile, drink her coffee, have a chat, what was her rush? But Em needed to be in Big Reed. "No offense, Suse, the coffee is delicious, but I gotta run. Communing with nature awaits and all that…"

"Here, take a snack then. You taking the blue path?"

" I was planning on blue today, yeah."

"Stick to brown. Just a feeling." Susan smiled. Em didn't miss the sign in her knowing green eyes.

Em parked the car and grabbed her Montauk sweatshirt and the little brown bag Susan gave her. She looked inside. Almonds and chocolate covered espresso beans. That Susan was a peach. Em looked at the sign on the split rail fence at the entrance to Big Reed. Monday, no hunting today. Nothing but babbling brooks and trees and Big Reed itself in all its glory. Em started out at the blue arrow on the tree and followed the path. She would switch to brown at the next turn. After she paid homage to her favorite tree.

Em had walked for a while. The huge oak was around the next bend. No hurry now. She stopped at the duck blind and sat down for a minute. She gazed out at Big Reed Pond. Geese flew overhead and a few bobbed in the water. So beautiful here. Em chewed an espresso bean and thought about her impending meeting with the Montauk Morality losers. She had an idea. She would ask Sin if she would let her take a half shift at Liars, for old times sake, and when the three holier than thou hypocrites showed their faces, which they undoubtedly would, she would tell them a little story while she poured their cocktails. The look on their faces would be just a beginning to the fun. They had no idea Em knew they hadn't cleaned up their act like the other members thought. It would be fun seeing them eat crow.

Em jumped when she heard the leaves crunch behind her. Silly, she thought, just animals in the woods. She got up and stretched and started to climb out of the duck blind when she heard a click. What the hell? There was no hunting today. But that was the distinct sound of a shotgun being pumped. Don't panic, she told herself, somebody didn't get the memo about no hunting on Monday. Idiot. "Hey, hello, hold your fire. No hunting today," Em shouted. Nothing.

The Appendage walked out of the reeds, a shotgun in her hand and a ridiculous kelly green scarf wrapped around her head. "Em."

"Are you for real? There's no hunting, today, didn't you read the sign?"

"Who said I was hunting? I followed you here."

"Why?" Em's palms were sweating but at the same time she was annoyed. The Appendage was stalking her?

"You shouldn't have told my husband where I was that night. None of your business, Em. Grunt and I had a real nice thing going. I *got* him. He *got* me. You ruined it all. Now I have no one. I am very angry."

"My heart bleeds for you. Listen, you are a married

woman. Grunt was playing with fire. So were you. You're lucky you weren't gutted yourself. Shooting me won't bring back Grunt or get your husband out of jail. Why don't you go to a spa and take a rest for awhile? Forget about men. I'm not your enemy. When you get back, guaranteed you'll feel better. Now empty the shells out of that thing and let's get out of here, the weather's taking a turn. Come on, I'll buy you a coffee at Susan's." *Maybe she has some arsenic in one of her jars.*

"I want to be a Mermaid. Will you hire me, Em?"

Give me strength. "How can I put this? There is sort of a cut off age. No offense."

"I'm too long in the tooth, is that it?"

"You said it, I didn't."

"What about the Admiral?"

"You want to sleep with Joey Flapjaws?"

"I'm lonely, Em. You don't understand my dilemma."

Oh brother. Em scratched her head. "Here, have an espresso bean." Em handed her the paper bag. She handed Em the shotgun and took the bag. " Okay, so you take a week at a spa somewhere, yes? Maybe in the Berkshires. Nice this time of year. When you get back, we'll talk about the Admiral." Em emptied the gun shells into her pocket. "Fair enough?"

"You're playing with me." The Appendage popped four espresso beans into her mouth.

"No, no I'm not. It turns out the Admiral's favorite Mermaid is leaving town. He's going to need some cheering up soon."

"Honest injun?"

Who talks like this? This injun would like to clock

you with this gun. "I stand by my word. I do have to tell you, the Admiral was sweet on his favorite Mermaid, so I can't promise he'll go for you."

"Oh he'll go for me all right. You have no idea what tricks I have up my sleeve, Em. There was this guy in Baja awhile back…he had never been tied up, so I…"

"Spare me the details. So you're handy with a scarf. Make it green. The Admiral's partial to it."

"You don't like me do you?"

"No flies on you. Listen, I'm just not into the girly chit chat."

"Not what I heard. You have those goddess parties. Rumor has it…"

"Listen, I don't give a fiddler's fart about some losers flapping their gums. Not that it concerns you, but I like men. Big seaworthy men."

"Grunt was big…I mean you never saw such a…well maybe you did?"

"I wasn't talking about that aspect. Never mind. And no we didn't."

"I miss him."

"I'm sorry."

"Why? You didn't kill him."

They reached the parking lot. Em noticed The Appendage's car, only now.

"I'll hang on to this, if you don't mind." Em placed the shotgun on her back seat.

"You said the Admiral likes green?" The Appendage adjusted her scarf and handed the bag of espresso beans to Em.

" Keep them. Is the pope Catholic? His daddy was reared in Dublin."

"Oh, good. I have a lot of green skirts. Scarves too. It could be fun."

" Well there you have it. See you in a week." Em sped off, leaving The Appendage to her dance of the seven green veils around the parking lot at Big Reed. Talk about being away with the fairies. Em clicked on the radio. Sugarloaf was singing Green Eyed Lady. Em laughed out loud.

Chapter Forty-Two

Shannie showed up first. Em had to contain herself when Shannie spotted her behind the bar. She grinned and Em wanted to slap her. "Lose your job, Em?" Shannie threw her coat on the empty table by the door and got herself cozy on a barstool for the night. She slapped down a pack of Marlboro Lights and a red lighter that said Hot Chick with orange flames on top of her smokes. She lit one and blew the smoke to the ceiling. Her pink lip gloss left a sticky imprint on the cigarette. Em tapped her fingers on the rubber bar mat. "I'm covering for Sin. Doing a favor for a good friend. What are you having?"

"Vodka cran, same as always. Quiet tonight. Where is everybody?"

"It's early. Place will be a zoo later. It's karaoke night."

"Shit, I forgot. Better play the jukebox while I can. Before the wailing and howling starts." She laughed at her own joke. Em didn't.

"They have some good singers actually."

"Give me a break."

Don't tempt me. Em put a drink in front of her. "This one's on me."

"Thanks. What for? We celebrating or something?"

"I thought we might do a little reminiscing, Shannie."

"I'm living in the moment now, Em. The past was a train wreck for me. I'd rather forget all that."

"But you had some juicy stories, Shan. Remember the adventures of Shannie and Dougie? That one

175

kept all of us on the edge of our seats. The time Mrs. Dougie walked in on the two of you, hot and heavy in the living room. She came home early from work and surprised the hell out of you guys. You said you were pumping away like rabbits and Dougie was rubbing Asti Spumanti all over your tits and …"

"Don't remind me. That was a bad day. Well, I mean it was a good day until his wife came home and lost her shit. Party pooper." Shannie laughed her classic naughty giggle. "Dougie was hot."

"And married."

"Unhappily."

"Get in line with that excuse."

"Why did you have to remind me about him? I'm all wet now. See what you did, Em? Now I need a shot. Make me a Lemonball will you? Wow. Dougie. I would jump that man if he walked in right now. You got no idea. We rocked it, Em."

"So much for living in the moment. You haven't changed a bit, Shannie. How did you convince those Montauk Morality Missionaries otherwise, I'm curious?"

Shannie threw back her shot and lit another cigarette. "Oh, so that's what this is all about?" She waved her hand around the bar. "You want me to leave your whore boat alone? All your little Mermaids."

"Exactly. And from your standpoint, you can surely see how we aren't hurting anyone."

"You saying I'm a whore?"

"If it walks like a duck…"

"Now you're being mean, Em. I can't help it if

married men like me. They can't resist me. What am I supposed to do? Refuse them?"

"Is that a rhetorical question?"

"What?"

"Never mind. Leave the Lily Virginia alone, Shannie. Get it?"

"Are you threatening me?"

"No. Leave my boat and my Mermaids alone. Screw whomever you like. I couldn't care less. Just don't interfere with my business and get your group off our back."

"I was trying to change, Em."

"Trying means not intending to change. You change or you don't. Simple. You are who you are, Shannie. Don't pretend to be something you're not. Hypocritical doesn't begin to…"

The door opened and slammed shut with the wind. "What is this, ladies night? Oh I take that back. What the hell is *she* doing here?" One of the locals looked Shannie up and down and sat at the opposite end of the bar. "Nice to see you though, Em. Can I have a OO7 please?" She glared at Shannie.

"What is her problem?" Shannie asked Em.

"Hello, you slept with her boyfriend."

"That was a long time ago, like last summer. Besides he bought me a drink. What was I supposed to do, say no?"

"A novel idea."

"You live in a dream world, Em."

Em placed the drink in front of her new customer. "Don't mind the party piece. She won't be here long. It's karaoke night."

"Oh Christ. I forgot."

Em poured a perfect Mudslide and handed it to one of the karaoke regulars. "This one's on me." The woman blew her a kiss and walked in the direction of the microphone to sing. Em sang along to Me And Bobby McGee while she pulled pints and made cocktails. "Nice voice, Em. You should sing one," Shannie told her.

"Never happen. You still here? I thought you couldn't stand karaoke."

"It's not bad, tonight. Besides I got nothing else to do. Hey, that guy's cute."

"He's married. Back off."

"You're no fun, Em." Shannie was on her feet, and working her way to the singer. She started a sexy little drunk dance on the wooden pole in front of him. He moved away and was singing to a woman at the table behind the pole. Shannie positioned herself in front of the woman and started her dance, this time touching the singer, who happened to be the DJ, on the neck and shoulder. He removed her hand and moved away again. Shannie tried once more and he reacted the same way. She finally threw her hands up dramatically, and walked over to the woman at the table. "What is his problem?"

"You. He isn't interested. It's obvious. Give it up."

"Oh yeah? Who the hell are you?"

"His wife."

"Well, you two should loosen up."

"Tell it walking, skank."

Shannie was about to open her mouth when Dragger grabbed her and turned her around. "Leave the lady be, Shannie."

"Well, look who graced us with his presence.

Slumming?"

"You should know. That's your specialty."

"Fuck you."

"Not even with his dick." Dragger pointed to Cal who just walked in the door with Jammin' Pam.

Dragger found a seat at the bar. "You come down to sing, Dragger?" Em put a Coke in front of him. "Maybe. I heard you were doing a cameo. How's it feel to be behind the bar again? Miss it? I see all your favorite people are here." Dragger laughed.

"I miss this like root canal. Oh look, the whore bride and her un-groom."

"Good one, Em. Let's fuck them up."

"What I had in mind was a little chat. Involving missionaries of a sort."

"Good deal. Why don't I sing War Pigs and get you in the mood?"

"I wait with bated breath." Em turned her attention to the couple made for each other, Arsenic and Sit On Your Face. "Hello, Pam. Hello, Cal," Em purred, "What can I get you? A little spoon and a lovin' spoonful?"

"Very funny, Em," Cal said.

"Yeah, I know what that means. And I don't swallow." The whore bride was insulted. Tante pis. Too bad.

"Too much information, Pam. Jack and Coke and Stoli O and soda?"

"Good memory, Em. What happened to your other job? You get a conscience?"

"You would be surprised at what I remember, Cal. And my conscience is clear, thanks.

Can't say the same yourselves, can you?"

Cal threw a twenty on the bar. Em pushed it back to him. "Keep your money. The first one's on me. For old time's sake."

"Why do I get the feeling there's a price attached?"

"No price, just a warning. Keep your moral morons away from my boat. You don't get to throw stones. Neither one of you. Deliver the message. Find another cause of the week."

Jammin' Pam pouted. "You got hookers on a boat, Em. Just because you call them Mermaids don't make it right." She took a long sip of her Stoli O and smiled at Cal like she had just delivered a profound statement to the world. Twiddle Dee and Twiddle Dum. Hopefully they never reproduce.

"Just because someone marries you, doesn't make you the princess bride, Pam. You're low hanging fruit. It's a wonder the CDC isn't called in after you sleep with your husband. Poor guy must have a standing refill at White's Pharmacy."

"You saying I'm dirty?"

"Is that a joke? You're a walking Petri dish."

"Em, that's enough. We didn't come here to be insulted." Now the Human Vacuum's feelings were hurt. The night was young and already it was priceless.

"Okay, Cal, then hear me. Keep your group away from my whore boat. We're staying. Otherwise, one phone call to my friend and you're fighting a coke charge bigger than your nostrils and the black hole beside you. Copish?"

"I know Teddie Tooker." That old peccadillo. Sergeant Teddie Tooker's name was spit out more than gum by more people in Montauk trying to talk their way out of a speeding ticket or a DUI.

"Big whoop. He knows you too. Shall we go any further?" Cal shut his mouth.

"Let's go, Cal." Jammin' Pam was bored.

"You have my word, Em. We're done with the boat. I swear."

"Thank you, Cal. Have a good night. Wear a condom." She winked.

"Generals gathered in their masses, just like witches at black masses...evil minds that plot destruction, sorcerers of death's construction..." Dragger was into it now. Em smiled as she wiped down the bar. He came over when he was done. "I almost coughed up a lung on that one. I'm too old for that fucking song." He downed his Coke and lit a cigarette.

" You? No way. They'll be playing that song at your funeral."

"You know something I don't? The grim reaper send you a message?"

Em laughed. "I was just saying. That song is you."

"Know what else is me? My bed. I'm out, Em. See you tomorrow."

" I hear Heaven is taking a little trip south via the River."

"Yep. We're down one Mermaid."

I know someone who asked to take her place."

"Who? Let's hear it."

"The Appendage."

Dragger laughed so hard, he thought he did cough up a lung this time. "That's fucking rich. The next thing you'll tell me is that she wants a date with the

Admiral."

"Actually his name did come up. She said she was lonely."

"You're giving me hives, Em, stop it."

"The Goddess's truth."

"On that note, I am gone. G'night."

"'Night, Dragger. Sweet dreams."

"Nightmares you mean. Thanks a lot." He shivered and headed for the door.

Chapter Forty-Three

"Can I be totally honest with you?"

"Ah, I hate when people say that, Em. Have you been less than honest with me all along? I am deeply hurt." Dragger stirred two sugars into his coffee. They were having breakfast at John's Pancake House on Main Street. "How are your pecan pancakes?"

"Great. I'm sorry, Dragger, really. From the bottom of my heart. It was for the greater good. Here it is. The Appendage's husband did not act alone."

"I knew it." He mopped up an over easy with his well done rye toast.

"You *did?*"

"Yeah. He ain't that sharp. So who rode shotgun that night? Don't keep me in suspense."

"Me."

"Right. And I am joining the priesthood."

I mean I paid him to get rid of our problem. I didn't specify how. The rest were his own demons acting out."

"Right. Years of being the Appendage's cuckold."

"Now there's a word you don't hear every day."

"I could have said pussy whipped, but I know how you hate that."

"Thanks, you are so considerate. There's more…"

"You and the Appendage's husband did the nasty?"

"Is everything about sex with you?"

"As opposed to?"

"Never mind. And no, not even close. You see he never found the money where I told him it would be. It is still there."

"*There* being?"

"Big Reed."

"You lost me."

Em explained how she made the deal with the Appendage's husband to get rid of Grunt. Get him out of town, take him on a long fishing trip, whatever. She said nothing about murder. Did she take advantage of his Achilles heel? Absolutely. Did that make her a bad person? Let's just say she wasn't going to win any humanitarian awards in this life.

The payoff was waiting for him in a tree at Big Reed. Dragger found this hilarious. "I suppose the Keebler elves are guarding it?" Em wasn't amused. "Only a few people know about the cache in a hole in the big oak tree in the old Montaukett settlement ruins." The cache being an old metal Army box filled with mostly notes and trinkets left by hikers. There was a trick to getting inside the box and the Appendage's husband knew it. Except he never claimed his prize because he ran for Hidden Lake instead of Big Reed and the rest was history.

Em was all set to get the stash until the Appendage, aka Annie Oakley, surprised her yesterday. Now that Dragger was up to speed, time was of the essence. And just in case the Appendage was still following Em, she thought Dragger should be the one to go get their money.

"Assuming it's still there," Dragger said, stamping out his cigarette.

"Oh it's there. Who else would take it?"

"You said the Appendage was hunting you the other

day."

"Very funny. She doesn't have the brains to figure it out. Dumb as a..."

"Rock," Dragger finished. "How come she knew you told her husband about herself and Grunt?"

"Lucky guess. Maybe he told her when she visited him in jail, I don't know. She didn't even have a purse that day I saw her. Where would she put all that money?"

"Now who's being du...?"

"Don't finish that. Just go and get our money. Please."

"Yes, m'lady." Dragger took a deep bow. "I sure hope you didn't underestimate the Appendage, Em."

"Me too," Em said under her breath. "Call me when you have it, okay?"

"Ten four."

Em bit a nail nervously. She had a sinking feeling she had made a dreadful mistake.

Chapter Forty-Four

If Em had considered confiding in Chase, her mind would have been eased. Dragger would not find the money Em hid in Big Reed because Chase already had. It all started the day she overheard Em telling Dragger she had a solution for getting rid of Grunt. She saw Em and the Appendage's husband, serious as undertakers in Em's car, outside of the Montauk Bake Shoppe, as she walked down from Willow to get a coffee. She put two and two together.

Chase knew all about the cache in Big Reed. Right after the Montaukett and the Talkhouse family, The Hookers were regulars in Big Reed. Granny Hooker took her on walks there all the time. She climbed up that big oak every single time and it was Granny herself who showed her the cache. They would leave a note for the next hikers to find. A little poem, a comment on their walk, or one of Granny's witticisms like: "I'm so sleepy I'm rum dumb."

Why did Chase interfere with Em's cache connection? Just a feeling something would go wrong and somebody other than the Appendage's husband would cash out. She had all intentions of giving Em the money, she just hadn't had the opportunity.

Dragger emptied the metal Army box. Nothing but a Ziploc bag with a bunch of junk inside. Trinkets people left behind. Key chains, toy figures, a pack of tissues, a Band-Aid, some seashells and pebbles, and a pencil and a small notebook. Kind of like a Big Reed guest book. People really needed to get a life. But no cashola. He shined a flashlight into the hole in the tree, in case Em decided to put the money in a bag and not the metal box. Nothing. Either the Appendage was sharper than he suspected or they had a little problem on their hands.

"Sorry, Em, the money is gone. My guess is the Keebler elves are on a bender. Maybe they took a trip to Blue Earth, Minnesota to visit the Little Green Sprout in his valley." Dragger leaned back in the chair in Em's office.

"Very funny. I won't ask why you know where the Little Green Sprout lives."

"My mind is an ever flowing font. Did you talk to Ass?"

"No, why? Does he have relatives in the valley of corn and peas?"

"Good one, Em. Just a hunch. Speak of the devil…"

Ass always knocked three knocks and two short ones. "Come in," Em said.

"Em, Dragger. What have we today? Any dilemmas? Incidentally, Chase is on her way."

"Hey, Ass, any idea where the money Em had in mind for the Appendage's husband went?"

"Are you saying we paid for that horrific murder?"

"No, Aspen," Em said. "I merely suggested to him that Grunt was involved with his wife. I thought he would take him on an extended boat trip. Killing was never discussed."

"So you raised a red flag in front of a bull? Then you paid the bull for his gore?"

"I didn't pay him. He never collected the money."

"Splitting hairs now are we?"

"Aspen may I remind you that it was you who shot Grunt?"

"He was merely grazed."

"So what's got your panties in a bunch, Ass? The money?"

"Well, yes. Sounds like we had a contract out on Grunt. Tell me I am wrong, Dragger."

"If we had the money, the whole thing would be moot," Em said.

"So where is it?" Ass wanted to know.

A light tapping of fingernails on the door. Chase. "Come on in," Em called out.

"Am I late for the meeting?" Chase brushed Aspen's lips and smiled at Em and Dragger.

"Just in time," Em said. "We're looking for some cash."

"Money does grow on trees after all, well, inside of them anyway." Chase put the bundle of bills on Em's desk.

"How did you…" Em scratched her head.

"I saw you that day outside the bakery. I knew the Appendage's husband wasn't going to do you any favors for free. When he ran to Hidden Lake, I acted quickly, ran to Big Reed. I know about the cache." Em smiled. "Of course you do."

"Sorry, I didn't mean to worry you. I was holding it for safekeeping. In case you were questioned and the boat searched."

"See? Problem solved. Well done, Chase." Aspen gave her a kiss.

"You are one smart cookie, Chase Hooker," Em said, smiling.

"Bravo, kiddo." Dragger adding his two cents.

"Thanks. Again, sorry for the worry."

There was a small complication remaining. The Appendage's husband. If he told the police he was paid to gut Grunt by the owners of the whore boat, they were all in acque calde. Then again, he was never paid for his handiwork and they had their money back, safe and sound.

Giving the Appendage a "job" as the Admiral's amusement would seal the deal. She would be more than happy to tell the police her husband was off his rocker and insanely jealous. The Appendage was a member of the Montauk Morality Mission, that is until they threw her out for being "even too weird for Montauk." Maybe her husband was trying to please her by getting rid of the whore boat's captain? That could be suggested. But so violently? Or maybe, he wanted the job for himself? That one had possibilities. These were questions worth pondering, Dragger thought, when he left Em's office. Anything to shine the light away from the whore boat. Maybe he needed another little meeting with the ex. Or would he do better to set his balls on fire? Some men never learn.

Chapter Forty-Five

"So I overheard two Saltys talking about one of your Mermaids. Her name is a spice. Not cinnamon, more exotic. Anyway, they were raving about her talents. Apparently she's double jointed and can …"

"Lake, spare me the details. I'm well aware of Saffron's forte. Glad the customers were pleased. Anyway, why the interest? Isn't that contradictory to your Montauk Morality mental cases group?"

They were sitting in Lake's trailer in Ditch Plains, drinking coffee. When Dragger called her that morning, she was more than accommodating, and invited him for coffee and bagels. Something was up, he thought, besides his dick. Even if he had gotten Lake out of his system, his johnson was holding on to the nostalgia. Hard.

Lake laughed, tucked an ashy blonde tendril behind her ear. "Truth is, I joined them as a spy. Don't tell anyone. You have to know I don't buy a word those bible thumpers have to say. They actually think I gave up my Buddhist beliefs and they saved my soul. What a hoot."

"Who exactly are you spying for?"

"The government."

"What?"

"*You,* jackass."

"Come again."

"Is that an invitation?"

Dragger shifted in his seat. He liked it better when Lake was clawing for him. What was up with the sweet talk? She wanted something. But what? She already took his balls years ago.

"Say something, you're making me nervous." Lake tapped her OM ring on her coffee mug.

"You nervous? Since when, Miss Serenity?"

"You haven't called me that in years. Mr. Delray, are you trying to seduce me?"

Down, boy. "Can we stick to the topic at hand? Why were you spying on those morons for me? I don't get it."

"Really? With all those Mermaids aboard, I would think you got it plenty…"

"Lake, knock it off. Answer the question. Now."

"Or what? You'll spank me?"

" Sure. Whatever rocks your boat. But not until you answer me."

"I did it for Chase."

"Okay, I'll bite. You spied on the moral morons because Chase asked you too?" Dragger had no idea what Lake was talking about. If he didn't know her better, he would think she was making this up as she went along. He braced himself for the punch line. He would never be ready for what he was about to hear.

"Dragger, I did it for Chase. She's our daughter."

"What are you talking about? Are you high? We have one daughter. And she isn't Chase." *She has a different name and I didn't sleep with her.*

"We had twins, Dragger. It's true. I knew beforehand, that's why I insisted on a midwife. Maybelle Hooker, Chase's granny. You were at sea, so the plan was perfect. Chase's mother was there instead. She wanted a child more than anything and couldn't have one of her own. We were friends. She didn't have many women friends. I gave her the baby born right after Tribeca. She called her Chase. She left town for a while and came back with her newly 'adopted' daughter. No one knew. Only she and I and Maybelle. We kept the secret all these years. Chase never has to know. I'm sorry you had to find out this way. Please say something."

Dragger just sat there staring at her. Lake was a little worried she had caused him some physical harm. "Dragger, I am telling you now because I was worried about Chase after that whole ugly business with Grunt. I couldn't sit back and let her be hauled off to jail with the rest of the whore boat. I was afraid she would be implicated somehow. And she wasn't even a Mermaid, thank the Goddess. Look, her mother is gone. And Maybelle too. I am the only one she has. And now she has you."

"She doesn't have me! Christ, Lake, what have you done? Do you realize…Jesus. Ah, what's the use? You don't get it…by the way, how did you know Chase was raped?"

"Oh my God! I didn't know. Who? Are you saying Grunt *raped* her?"

"Yeah I'm saying that. For Christ's sake, Lake, why do you think we got rid of him?"

"*You* killed him?"

"I wanted to, yes. But, no, none of us killed him. The Appendage's husband is the murderer. You read the papers. Never mind that. Lake, for crying out loud, you don't know the half of it… I…"

"No you didn't. Do not tell me you slept with our daughter?"

"Are you the devil incarnate? How can you talk like that?"

"I'm not the one who slept with her."

"Stop saying that. I didn't know she was my... this is too damn much. I can't fucking deal with this." Dragger started rummaging through Lake's kitchen cabinets. Drawers went flying open, a tower of Tupperware falling all over the tile floor. "Where do you hide it?"

"Get a grip, Dragger. There's no booze in there. I gave it up for Lent. Breathe, for God's sake. Calm yourself. You've had a shock."

Dragger opened the door and stepped outside the trailer. He walked down the steps and sat in a chair facing the ocean. The sea breeze brushed his cheek. He lit a cigarette and exhaled a stream of anger.

Lake brought two cups of coffee outside. She handed one to Dragger.

"You're imperfect, Dragger. Welcome to the club."

He looked at her sideways. "Really? That's the best you got? Is your young stud our third child? Christ, how the hell would you know how I feel? You should have told me, Lake. We were married. Not supposed to have secrets. Does Tribeca know?"

Lake shook her head. "Don't go down the truth path with me, Dragger. Your record is shot to hell. Yes, I, Miss 99 and one tenths percent pure made a mistake. Granted, a big one. And what would be the point of telling Tribeca? Chase is her best friend. I wouldn't interfere with that relationship. I promised her mother."

"You're just the little keeper of the Holy Grail aren't you? St. Lake."

Lake let that one go. She knew her ex-husband better than anyone. They drank their coffee in silence. The waves crashed to shore, their presence a third party spilling unspoken words.

"Now you know why I joined the Montauk Morality Mission," Lake said softly.

"Who cares about those idiots now? I am so mad, I swear I could..."

"Beat the shit out of me? I know I deserve it. But "Ex Bar Brawler Slugs Buddhist," wouldn't look good in the Star's headlines next week."

"Don't be cute. Oh man, could I use a drink right now. Buddhist bitch."

"Stop it. You don't drink anymore. And you're stronger than a little truth. I gave a lonely woman a gift. Buddha would say I was generous of spirit. I have no regrets. What would we have done, drag two young girls through a divorce? Things turned out the way they were supposed to. Apart from you and your insatiable urges. I forgave *you.* Why don't you come back inside, let me give you a backrub and we'll call it even? We won't speak of this again. Deal?"

"Why don't you fuck Buddha? You're not right, you know that? Why did you tell me, Lake? I could have gone peacefully to my grave an ignorant bastard. Thanks for nothing."

"You asked, remember? You asked why I was so concerned for Chase," Lake said, dropping her jeans and stepping out of her panties.

"Come on, that's not right." *Why did she still have*

to have that amazing body? Those awesome breasts. Nipples smelled like peaches. Not right, man. I'm toast.

"It isn't right did you say? Then how come your cock is hard?"

"What kind of Buddhist are you?"

"The other kind." Lake smiled.

Dragger locked the trailer door and followed Lake into her bedroom.

Chapter Forty-Six

"Well I must say that was a version of Cooley's Reel I haven't had the pleasure of hearing, well, seeing really. With the veils and all. Thank you, Miss…"

"Your welcome, Admiral. Call me Bridget O'Malley," the Appendage said.

"Like the song? Sad one that. *Oh Bridget O'Malley, you left my heart shaken with hopeless desolation, I'd have you to know.*"

"Nice, Admiral. Can I tell you a secret?"

"Why of course, my dear. Would you perhaps like to do another dance first?"

"In a minute. I just need to get something off my chest. You must not breathe a word now. Promise?" The Appendage sat on the Admiral's lap and stroked his beard.

"Fire away, Bridget O'Malley." The Admiral smiled, touching her breasts. He was feeling quite excited. He must remember to thank Em for his new visitor. She was no comparison to Heaven, but the flesh is weak. Heaven would never begrudge him a little pleasure.

"I know who killed Grunt," she whispered in the Admiral's ear as she tied one of his arms to the headboard with her green scarf.

"Of course you do. The Appendage's husband. We all know that."

"No, someone made it look like it was him. Put that knife in his truck."

"And you know this person, Bridget?"

The Appendage tied his other arm to the headboard.

"Yes. But she's not going to confess."

The Admiral was having trouble concentrating. "Um, Bridget dear, I don't think a woman could be capable of such violence, let alone the way Grunt was well, gutted like a fish, rest his soul." He looked into Bridget O'Malley's eyes. She was straddling him now. Her eyes had a peculiar vacancy about them. Sad woman, he imagined. Like the song.

"She could have if she was a fisherwoman. Knew her way around a boat and all."

The Appendage removed her panties and sat on the Admiral again. "What do you think, Admiral?"

"I think we should sing. *Oh Bridget O'Malley, you left my heart shaken, with a hopeless desolation, I'd have you to know. It's the wonders of admiration your quiet face has taken. And your beauty will haunt me wherever I go.*"

The Appendage removed the Admiral's pants and rode him. She sang a different song while the Admiral panted and hummed 'Bridget O'Malley.' "*She gutted 'ol Grunt when he took that young Mermaid. I gave him my body and soul and attention, he used me and gave that young Mermaid his all. I miss him, that big man, but now he is ashes. Never to come to me, come to me, come to me ....*"

"I'm coming," the Admiral said, "Brace yourself, Bridget."

"Me too, Admiral, confessions make me horny."

"Have you something to confess, Bridget O'Malley?" the Admiral asked as they lay side by side.

"No, never mind. Sing me that song again."
"Oh Bridget O'Malley, you left my heart shaken…"

Chapter Forty-Seven

Dragger and the Admiral were alone in the wheelhouse. Mermaid business was being conducted below. Em was keeping the waiting johns amused with stories of the Montauketts in the salon. Chase was giving the Appendage a massage. Aspen was planning how he was going to pop the question to Chase. It was a clear crisp October night. The bombshell that Lake dropped in Dragger's lap continued to rattle him, but he was managing to keep his emotions under a boil.

"Dragger, my boy, what would make someone who was not guilty of a crime run anyway? In your humble opinion."

"Are we talking about a specific person, Admiral? Or is this a hypothetical thing?"

"Let's say the Appendage's husband did not do it after all, and it was a woman who committed the crime."

"Hey, hold your horses there, what woman are we speaking of?"

"I don't know exactly. Only that Bridget O'Malley said she knew who the woman was but she would never say."

"Who the hell is Bridget O'Malley?"

"The woman with the scarves that Em sent to my cabin. We had a grand time, we did."

"The Appendage? She told you a woman gutted Grunt?"

"No, Dragger, I told you, Bridget O'Malley whispered in my ear. Well we were in a delicate position and she sort of sang it out. I may be on in years, but I don't miss a trick."

Dragger lit a cigarette. He took a hard pull and exhaled. "Are you saying the Appendage, who now calls herself Bridget O'Malley, what is that all about? Some kind of game you were playing? Who were you? Captain Ahab? Never mind. So she told you *she* killed Grunt. Not her husband? This is very important information you've uncovered, Admiral. I mean I knew she was a nutbag, excuse me, a little unstable, but this is rich. And what do we do about it?"

"I believe we do nothing about it. I was a priest, you understand. So in a way, her confession is between Bridget and myself. By the way, I would never take a demotion to Captain. Game or not."

" Right, I hear you on that. Okay, so this confession is sacred you're saying? But you just told me. Why?"

"Because we go way back, Dragger, and I know you honor the fisherman's code."

"We're talking about murder, Admiral."

"Yes, my boy, so we are. However, murder of the man who raped Chase."

Dragger winced. That one he took full brunt. His gut was leaking. He found himself momentarily speechless. What was that karma shit Lake was always yapping about? Anybody else want to have a go at old Dragger today?

"Dragger, I realize I have hit a major nerve. I am so sorry."

"You know much more than the Appendage, um, Bridget O'Malley's confession, don't you?"

"I've lived in this town all my life. Maybelle

Hooker was a very good friend. Very good, you understand. I walk on the rug she made me every morning."

"Chase's grandmother? You're quite the stud. More pillow talk? What do you do to these women? Jesus."

The Admiral laughed. A hearty chuckle. "I am a good listener. All those years in the confessional. Please don't take the Lord's name in vain. I know you are upset."

"Upset? In one day I find out I have another daughter and the guy in jail for Grunt's murder is not the one who did it, but now we have a killer on the boat. You're fucking straight I'm upset. Excuse my French."

"At least you have Lake to console you now."

"Okay, now you're starting to scare me, Admiral. How the hell do you know about me and Lake?"

"I told you, I listen. She has the most lovely peace signs in her little store, don't you think? Gentle soul she is. Like a ray of light."

"I need a fucking drink."

"No. That is what we do not need. Neither of us. Now go get us a nice cup of coffee and a chocolate bar and we can talk some more. Mums the word."

"Apparently mum is not the word. Who else knows about any of this?"

"Just you and I and Bridget O'Malley."

"Well keep her quiet, Admiral. Until I can think of our next move."

"No worries, she'll be nice and relaxed after her massage. Probably take a nap."

"What? She's with Chase right now?" Dragger's

head was starting to pound. Why did he give up the weed? A nice joint would go down smoothly right about now.

"Bridget won't tell Chase. You can count on it."

Dragger was afraid to ask. "And why is that?

"Be assured, Dragger, you have nothing to worry about. After our delightful romp, I told Bridget O'Malley if she breathes another word about Grunt or anything else, she is off the boat for good."

" And you think that's enough of a threat?"

"I do. She has nowhere else to go. Her husband's boat was repossessed. She can't make the rent on her house. Bridget will stay with me when we're ashore."

"You need that headache?"

"Bridget O'Malley has shown me a very good time. I like her very much. I knew Heaven was only a fleeting moment. You wouldn't take this happiness from me, would you?"

Dragger scratched his head. Lake was right though he hated to admit it. Men and their balls. It doesn't get more simple than that. No matter the age.

" 'Course not, Admiral. Rock on. I'm going below for those coffees."

"Don't forget the nut bars."

Dragger laughed. "As if I could."

Chapter Forty-Eight

"Sit down Ass, I need to talk to you," Dragger said. They were in Dragger's place in the Harbor. "Coffee all right? I don't have any Earl Gray."

"Coffee will do, thank you. Sounds ominous. I thought we had a good run this week. Books look good. Mermaids are happy. Clients as well, obviously. All return johns. So what's on your mind?"

"Do you think I'm a bad guy, Ass? I mean, as far as assholes go, am I at the top of the list?" Dragger set a mug in front of Aspen.

Aspen took a sip of coffee. "This will put hair on my chest. Very robust indeed."

"Ass, I need an answer."

"Sorry. Right. No, I do not believe you to be an asshole at all. And since when do you care what people think? What is causing this self reflection? Have you and Lake had a row?"

"Oh brother, does everyone know I'm bonking my ex? Jesus."

"Sorry. Chase mentioned it. I wouldn't breathe a word of course. Neither would she."

Aspen noticed at the mention of Chase's name, Dragger went a little pale. He was fidgeting with his cigarette pack. "Is it Chase then?"

"Is what Chase?"

"The reason you called me here? Is something the matter with her? Is there a problem?"

Dragger got up and looked out the window. Late afternoon boats were heading in.

"Chase is great. I'm too old for revelations, that's all."

"Who has revealed themselves? Excuse me, but I am at a loss here."

"Not your fault, Ass. My ex wife has a cruel sense of timing, that's all."

"Are we talking about the Montauk Morality Mission? I understood Em had taken care of them? I do know Lake was instrumental as far as a covert fishing expedition shall we say."

Dragger laughed, unpleasantly. "Yeah, Lake is real good at keeping secrets. No, the M&M's are off our back, I know that. Don't mind me, I'm just fucked up from the ex. My own fault. Letting the little head lead."

"If I may say, don't be too hard on yourself, Dragger. You're only human. You have a daughter together." Again that wounded look in Dragger's eyes.

"You mean Tribeca?"

"Of course. Who else? If I may say so, you're acting very odd."

Dragger blew out a breath. Okay, so Chase's heredity wasn't public knowledge. "That's me, an old odd fuck. You know what? Let's change the subject."

"Right. How would you feel about giving Chase away? I asked her to marry me."

So much for changing the subject. "Why me?"

"Her father is dead. She would be honored if you would say yes. We both would."

Dragger scratched his face. He needed a shave. "How could I say no?"

"Brilliant. And Dragger? Chase has no regrets or blame. Neither should you."

"Excuse me?" Holy fuck, she told Ass about them?

"What I mean is, she doesn't regret coming aboard our boat. She says if not for you, she wouldn't have met me. We both owe you the world for that."

"You know what, Ass? You're all right."

"We're partners, mate. I don't take that lightly."

"Thanks, Ass."

"For what?"

"A bit of redemption."

Chapter Forty-Nine

"The Appendage's husband is free," Sin announced as she sprayed Windex on the bar. It was two in the afternoon and Liars was quiet as a morgue. Even the Jukebox was off. The television on mute with the Weather Channel. A few boats remained in their slips out front. The day was perfect for fishing. No wind, water clear as glass.

"Are you kidding me?" Dragger blew out a stream of smoke. "On bail? How?"

"He says he didn't do it. Apparently they found other prints on his fishing knife. Teddie Tooker's looking to have a word with the Appendage. Rumor has it she's on your boat."

Dragger shook the ice in his Coke, downed the rest of it. Sin refilled his cup.

"Yeah, so what? She's keeping the Admiral busy. Go figure."

Sin laughed her loud belly cackle. "That's a picture I don't need."

"Me either, but it keeps the Admiral happy. What do you think about her? Is she capable of that mess made of Grunt?"

"Ever see her filet a fish? Kind of creepy, the way she moves the knife. Precision for sure, but like there's some pleasure involved. Let's just say, I wouldn't want to piss her off. And I hear Grunt did."

"What exactly did you hear?"

"Grunt threw her over for some Mermaid. They had a fight here one night. She was crying, he told her to get over it. None of her business and all. She wasn't happy."

"I don't get how she knew about...Grunt never would have told her. I have to think someone..." Dragger realized he was thinking out loud. He lit another cigarette and stood up to leave.

"Dragger? You were saying? Knew about who?"

"Nothing, nothing. Sorry, Sin, I gotta go. Boat business. Thanks for the Coke. And the info."

"Yep. Thanks for the company. And for not finishing the damn story."

"Sin, some day, we'll talk. Not today."

"Right. Get going. I got work to do." She laughed.

Dragger sat in his truck. He checked his speed dial and hit a button. "Montauk Police."

"Captain Tooker, please."

"Who's calling?"

"Dragger Delray."

"Is he expecting your call?"

"Yep," Dragger lied.

"Hold on."

"Dragger. What can I do for you?"

"Hey Teddie, can I talk to you somewhere in private?"

"Does this have to do with the Appendage's husband by any chance?"

"Yeah. I have some information."

"That so? Meet me at Fort Hill in half an hour."

"Thanks, Teddie. Appreciate it."

"I didn't do anything. But you're welcome."

Dragger smiled and clicked off his phone.

They sat on the bench overlooking the water up at Fort Hill Cemetery. Council Rock, the big quartz boulder that was there when the Montaukett

Indians used to meet centuries ago glittered in the sun. The Montauketts buried some of their dead up at Fort Hill and people say you can feel their presence.

"Shoot, Dragger," Teddie Tooker said.

Dragger smiled. Funny words coming from a cop. "I hear you're looking at the Appendage for Grunt's murder?"

"Maybe. Her husband claims he's not our man."

"Teddie, I gotta ask you a big favor."

"I'm not going to like this, am I?"

"Probably not. But here it is. Say she did it. She gutted Grunt like a fish. It didn't dawn on me at first. I forgot how handy she was with a filet knife. Too bad Grunt didn't cop on sooner. Anyway, what if she did everyone a favor?"

"Come again?"

"He raped Chase." The words still made Dragger wince. This didn't go unnoticed.

"Sounds personal."

"It's not," he lied. "Look, Teddie, she's a nice kid. He took advantage of her. She wasn't a Mermaid. He knew that. We were gonna get rid of him. Not kill him. Just send him away. The Appendage's husband agreed to take him down south somewhere. Anywhere. Just get him off the boat and away from Chase. Then the Appendage took matters into her own hands. We knew nothing of that until…"

"Go on…"

"Until she sang to the Admiral."

"This just gets better and better. You got Flapjaws on the boat now?"

"Yeah. He's fine, believe it or not. And the

Appendage keeps him happy."

"God Bless him. But what do you expect me to do? Forget what you just told me?"

"Yeah. Yeah, Teddie."

"Here's the thing, Dragger. Maybelle Hooker was my great aunt. Yep. No lie. Bet you didn't know that. Not a lot of people do. So I know exactly where all this is coming from, Dragger."

Dragger lit a cigarette. *How many other people knew Chase was his daughter?*

"So you understand what I'm asking. Can you do this or not, Teddie?"

"Done. But I have to bring the Appendage in for questioning. If we get her to say Grunt threatened her or bragged heartlessly about Chase and she lost it, went ballistic on him…I think she'll cooperate and we won't have a scandal. I can't very well have a female Dexter running around Montauk. Hey, I hear the M&M's are on your back?"

"Yeah. Assholes. Listen, I appreciate this, Teddie. I can't tell you how much. Chase is getting married and I'm father of the bride it turns out. In name only, of course."

"I doubt that." Captain Teddie Tooker shook Dragger's hand and walked down the hill to his unmarked truck. Dragger stayed put for a few minutes. He needed to gather himself before he went to see Em.

Chapter Fifty

Chase uncorked a bottle of Pinot Noir from Duck Walk Vineyards. Her friend's favorite. She unwrapped a triangle of Brie and set it out on a pretty saucer from her Granny Maybelle's collection. A basket of water crackers with a nice cloth napkin and some Kalamata olives in a small lime green bowl completed her little spread. She uncorked the wine and lit the fire.

The door bell rang. She was always on time. "Hey you," Chase said. "Come on in. Good to see you."

"Good to be seen," Tribeca said. "Now pour me some wine and let's get cozy. I love this cottage. It makes me feel interesting, you know what I mean?"

Chase laughed and handed Tribeca a glass of wine. "You are interesting. But I know what you mean. Like you're in an old movie. Doilytown."

Tribeca laughed. "Exactly. And Rag Rug village. You miss Granny Maybelle, don't you?"

"Every day. I have some questions for her…" Chase looked into the fire.

"So how is that Aspen of yours? When do I get to meet him?"

Subject expertly changed. "Soon, Tri, I promise. You know Granny wouldn't have approved of what we did. She brought life into the world, she didn't destroy it…"

Tribeca thoughtfully chewed a Brie covered cracker and took a slow sip of her wine.

"Chase, we did what we had to do. Stop agonizing over it, okay? It's done, sweetie."

Tribeca, ever the cool headed one. She got that from Lake. *What did I get*? Chase wondered.

"How can you be so nonchalant about it? Aren't you the least bit afraid Dragger will find out?"

"You're talking about my father, who thinks I think he runs a party boat that is strictly for fishing?"

"Don't be cute. He isn't stupid, Tri."

"I know. But didn't you hear? The Appendage confessed. Case closed."

"Not necessarily. If Teddie Tooker picks this apart, and he will, there are holes in her story. She confessed to the Admiral. Give me a break. Teddie isn't an idiot."

"Chase, are you trying to borrow trouble? In a million years, Dragger and Teddie Tooker are not going to suspect *us*."

"Really? Don't be so sure. Your father already mentioned our filleting skills once at Em's. In fact he referred to us winning that contest down at the docks. See? His mind is not at rest."

"Okay, fair enough. Say he is suspicious and knows in his heart of hearts that the Appendage didn't do it. He is not truly going to think you or I had anything to do with Grunt's murder. Come on. I had dinner with Dragger that night and flew back to California."

"But you didn't. You were here with me until we…"

"You are reaching, Chase. Leave it. What we know, Dragger will never figure out. And just say he does, what do you think he would do with such information anyway? Turn his own daughters in?

Never. He would keep it in his head forever."

Chase winced. "*You're* his daughter. The surgeon. I'm the whore boat masseuse. He doesn't know about me, remember. I'm the dirty family secret. Thanks, Granny." Chase held her wineglass up to her Granny Hooker's framed picture over the mantle.

"Knock it off, Chase. Are you feeling sorry for yourself? Dragger cares for you, you have to know that. If he ever found out that you were his daughter, he would..."

"Shoot himself?" Chase interrupted. "Trust me, Tri, You have no idea. Let's change the subject." Now it was her turn to be evasive. Tribeca could never know that Dragger and Chase slept together once. That secret would stay buried. It had to.

"Fine. Just so long as you stop obsessing about what can't be undone. Chase?"

"Okay, okay. No talk about murder."

"It was self-defense."

"After the fact."

"He raped you."

"Thanks for reminding me. We planned it, Tri."

"Boy, you are going to beat this dead horse, aren't you?"

"Tri, I'm not sleeping well."

"I'll write you a scrip for some light sleeping pills. Or why not take some Valerian. It's natural. Granny would have advised that, wouldn't she?"

"Granny's not here."

"What in the world has gotten into you? Never mind, I know what this is about, you're getting hitched. You've got a case of the bitchy bride doldrums."

"Fuck off."

"Okay, I deserved that one. Sorry. You miss your mother, is that it?"

"Which one?"

"Ouch. Touché,' little sis."

"We're twins."

"I popped out first."

"Bitch."

"That's better. Chase, seriously, what can I say to make you feel better? I hate this."

"Tell me that we'll be okay. Tell me we didn't carve that asshole up like a giant tuna. Tell me Dragger will never find out about me. Tell me why Lake gave me away."

"Number one, we will be fine. Two, yes we did get rid of Grunt and he deserved it. Let it go. We saved the state money to keep him locked up. He was raping women, Chase. Get your head around that and then clear your mind of it. Three, Dragger knows nothing about your birth and that's the way it stays. Lake will see to it. And speaking of my mother, she gave you to your mom. She wanted a baby. Maybelle agreed to keep their secret. Chase, I love you. We always knew, didn't we? Deep down? We were too alike in so many ways to be only the best of friends."

Chase wiped her eyes. "I didn't know… not until I found Lake's letter to my mother a few days ago. I was looking for old family pictures in the attic, to show Aspen. That's a joke. Who the hell am I, Tri? I just can't help feeling, I could have been *more*…"

"More than what? You are you. An amazing woman, Chase."

"You're a doctor. That means something."

"You are a skilled physical therapist and masseuse. And you're beautiful. And everyone loves you."

"Blah, blah, looks fade."

"Well then you can slip into your old waders and drop a line in the water. Be an old sea hag in your twilight years. Write a book about the Mermaids."

"I hate you."

"You do no such thing. I adore you, sis."

"Me too. Sorry. I am a whining brat today. Forgive me?"

"Of course," Tribeca kissed her. "So tell me about the boat. Any new Mermaids?"

"Yep. Her name is Luna. Dark hair, legs up to here… and she dances."

"On a pole?"

Chase laughed. "No, not on a pole. She has all these energetic dance moves. She used to be an aerobics teacher. She can stand on her head too."

"I get the visual. Handy. Do you worry about Aspen with these hot chicks on the boat?"

"Not at all. Aspen is as straight as an arrow. Loyal as they come. And for some reason that I have yet to understand, he is crazy about me. Imagine."

"Smart man."

"I lucked out the day I met him. That horrible day that turned into … Aspen was the amazing one. I thought he fell from the sky, Tri. I never met a man like him."

"You deserve it."

"How's Peter?"

"He's great. Even keel all the way. He's busy unwrinkling and unsagging the rich and famous."
Chase laughed. "You love him still?"
"I adore the guy. He puts up with me. He is a saint."
"True. No, seriously, what did you ever do? I mean you are bossy..."
        Tribeca stuck out her tongue. "By the way, what is up with Lake and my father?"
Subject changed. Chase left it alone. "You know Dragger, he pretends he hates Lake with a passion and at the same time he can't keep away from her."
"Thin line between love and hate," Tribeca said.
"Exactly."
"So are we good, Chase? Ugly business adjourned?"
"Yep. Over. Are you hungry?"
"Is the sea blue?"
"Let's eat."
"You're not feeding me kale, are you? I eat enough greens in Cali to turn into the Incredible Hulk."
Chase laughed. "Babyback ribs, hot barbeque sauce, smashed red potatoes with butter, and butterscotch sundaes for dessert. Is that radical enough, Doc?"
"Heaven. Bring it on. Hey, you mind if I close the window? It's getting chilly."
"Suit yourself," Chase said, dishing out their feast on two large plates.

Chapter Fifty-One

"Did you hear that?" Chase stopped wiping the table. Tribeca was at the sink up to her elbows in suds. "Hear what?"

"I heard something outside," Chase said.

"It's just the wind. There's a nor'easter headed this way. I heard it on the radio earlier. Good thing you have lots of candles." She went back to rinsing a dish.

"There it is again..." Chase went to the window and looked out. Pitch black. She turned on the backyard light. Everything was exactly as she left it that afternoon. Her garden rake was leaning against the shed. Empty flower flats were stacked next to it.

"Come on, let's go out and have a look around," Tribeca said, wiping her hands on a dish towel. "I swear you just heard the wind."

Chase grabbed a sharp knife out of the drain board. She threw a shawl around her shoulders. "Ready."

"What are you doing with that? Planning on...never mind."

Chase stood over the garden under the living room window. "See? Footprints. Not mine." A few early daffodils blew in the wind, next to them, two small fresh footprints. "They're not mine. Tri?"

"I heard you." Tribeca walked towards the front of the cottage. The wind was whipping up a good pace stronger. "Whoever was here is gone, Chase. Let's get the hell inside. I'm freezing."

Tribeca poured them a brandy. "Drink this, we're okay. No one is out there."

"Should I call the police?" Chase put the knife in

the drawer.

"And say what? There was a gnome in your garden?"

"Very funny. Who the hell would be spying on me?"

"The Admiral maybe. He likes you."

"Shut up."

"Look, let's go to bed. Lock up. I'm going up to put my jammies on."

Chase clicked the deadbolts on both doors and left a lamp on in the kitchen. She took extra candles upstairs and a lighter. Granny's shotgun was in the upstairs closet. Tribeca was propped up on pillows drinking her brandy, all snug in her pj's. "Uh, Annie Oakley, is that thing loaded?"

"Yep."

"Good. Now get in here and let's get some shut eye."

"Who are you, John Wayne?"

"You're the one with the gun."

Chase laughed and set the shotgun next to her side of the bed. "I'll be right in, I have to brush my teeth."

"I'll be on the lookout, partner."

"Great. You're very threatening in your silk long johns."

"Hey, I live in San Diego, my blood's thinned."

"Sad. My sister the mush."

Tribeca threw a slipper at her. It missed Chase and hit the door. Chase hooted. "I hope you can shoot straighter than that."

Chase got under the covers and sipped her brandy. "I'm glad you're here, Tri."

"Me too. I have a surprise for you. Want to hear it?"
"Then it won't be a surprise, will it? Okay, I'm all ears."
"Peter can fix that."
"Fuck off."
Tribeca laughed. "Your ears are perfect. Anyway, I'm taking you to Canyon Ranch for a few days, as a maid of honor gift. Don't say no."
"That's expensive, Tri."
"I'm a doctor."
"Show off."
"When do we leave?"
"That's the spirit. Can you get away from the boat next week?"
"I'll talk to Em. I'm sure she'll be cool with that. I can't wait to get out of here. But won't it look suspicious, me leaving town? You too."
       "No. It's your pre-wedding girl's getaway. And I don't live here, remember? Stop stressing. Think massages, treatments, hikes, swimming, good food, wine."
"Do they serve wine at a spa?"
"If they don't we'll smuggle some in. What about Aspen? Will he mind you leaving?"
"Aspen isn't needy. That's why I love him."
"Wise girl."
"How about Peter? Won't he miss you?"
"He's a big boy. Plus he has a nip and tuck conference out in LA next week."
"Are you two ever in the same place at the same time?"
"Just enough to keep us on our toes. Peter is a cakewalk. And he puts up with me. Believe me, he

was used to California women. They are so laid back they're nearly comatose. I stirred him up and he likes that. That edge."

"He has no idea how edgy we Montauk girls can be…"

"Night, sis."

"Night Tri."

Chapter Fifty-Two

Em stamped the dirt off her shoes and unlocked her front door. SoCo and Lime meowed around her legs. "Hungry babies? Mommy has your food." Em put her purse down on the counter and reached under the sink for the sack of Meow Mix. She was thinking about a nice tall gin and tonic. She filled the cat's bowls and hit the button on her voice mail. One from Teddie Tooker. One from Dragger. Dragger's sounded urgent.

She punched in his number and filled a glass with ice.

"It's your dime..."

"I'm home now, what's up?"

"Not on the phone, Em."

"Come on over."

"I'm outside."

"Then come on in. I'll put up some coffee."

Dragger let himself in the kitchen door. "Hey."

"Hey yourself. Coffee will be done in a minute."

"I got something eating at me, Em."

"Spill it."

Dragger fidgeted with his cigarette pack.

"Go ahead, smoke," Em said. "Take a load off. What's going on?"

Dragger sat by the fireplace. He blew the smoke up the chimney. "This Appendage business is giving me agita."

"You talking about her and the Admiral?" Em reached for a large mug on a shelf over the stove.

"Nah, Flapjaws don't bother me. He's happy and sober, so we're cool. I just don't see her gutting

Grunt all by herself."

"What about the husband?" Em handed Dragger a black coffee.

"Thanks. I definitely don't see him doing it. The guy's not the type. Jealous maybe, but not too sharp or strong. Basically harmless."

Em rolled up a bit of The Star and lit a match. The kindling she had laid for a fire caught and crackled. She sat down across from Dragger. And sipped her gin.

"Dragger, what if I told you I thought you would be better off leaving this alone?"

"And why is that?" He tapped his coffee mug.

"Huge can of worms will fall on your head."

"Can't be any worse than what's been happening lately."

"Want to bet?"

"Now you got my attention. Your turn to spill the beans."

Em reached for Dragger's cigarettes. "Mind?"

"Help yourself. Get to the story, Em."

"Patience is not your strong suit."

" Really? You're the first person to say that."

Em laughed. "Okay, but I don't want to do this. It is against my better judgment."

"Oh shit…" Dragger sat back and blew a stream of smoke to the ceiling.

"You're right about the Appendage. But Teddie Tooker doesn't know anything more. He doesn't know Chase was raped for instance."

Dragger shifted in his chair. "He sort of does know."

"That's not good. But still, if he thinks the Appendage killed Grunt in a jealous rage with or without her husband or someone else, Chase is off the hook."

"I wasn't aware she was on the hook. What's the deal, Em? Chase talk to you?"

"No. Nothing like that. I just put two and two together that's all."

"And what'd you get? And don't say four."

"You don't want to know, Dragger. I really think you should leave it alone."

"Too late for that. I asked you what the story was, are you gonna tell me or what?"

Em got up and stirred the fire. "You don't make this easy."

"Easy ain't in my vocabulary. Talk, Em, you're giving me more agita."

"I hate being the bearer of bad news. I just don't want you to hear it from anyone else."

"Who else knows?"

"No one, honest. It's just a theory of mine right now. But just in case it comes true, you should be warned."

"Christ, Em, what the fuck?"

"All right. All right. It's Chase. It was Chase. *She* killed Grunt."

Dragger laughed out loud. "Chase carved up Grunt? That's priceless. Even if Ass helped her, which he never would, he's squeamish, that's ridiculous."

"Why? You accused her at my house. Remember?"

"I wasn't serious, Em."

"Well I think it's true. And she had help. And it wasn't Aspen."

"Okay, Jessica Fletcher, I'll bite. Who?" Dragger got up to get a coffee refill. Em mixed herself another gin and tonic. She needed it.

"Someone near and dear to you."

"What? Come on. Lake is a Buddhist. The two occasions we had sex lately, doesn't exactly make her near and dear to me."

"I wasn't talking about Lake…"

"Then who else? There's nobody that dear I care about except…"

"Sit down, Dragger."

"I'm fine where I am." He stood stubbornly flat footed leaning on the kitchen counter.

"Okay. You're not gonna like this one bit." Em took a sip of her drink and lit another of Dragger's cigarettes.

"Christ, just spit it out." Dragger was working on a migraine and his gut was leaking big time.

Em nodded. "Once upon a time there were two girls. Best friends. Almost like sisters. One stayed in Montauk, the other left. But before they parted they had this amazing summer and entered the fish filleting contest…"

"Don't go there, Em. No fucking way. You telling me my daughter, a doctor for crying out loud, sliced up Grunt for sushi? And Chase helped? The sister murderers of Montauk? Fuck that, Em."

"I said they were best friends, not sisters."

"They *are* sisters. Blood. Yeah, ain't that just ducky? Thanks to my fucking "we are the world" ex-wife and goddamn Maybelle Hooker."

Em almost choked on her gin. "Holy crap. I didn't know, Dragger. But now that you mention it, it makes perfect sense. Oh my God..."

"What do you mean it makes sense? Fucking nothing makes sense. Fuck, I need a goddamn drink." He reached for the bottle of gin. "This all you got? No whiskey? No Jack?"

"Jack died as far as you're concerned, and you're not getting a drop of booze from me. Don't give me that look. Coffee and chocolate, that's what I have. Sorry, Dragger."

"Bitch."

"Deal with it. I'm truly sorry about Tribeca and Chase."

Dragger rubbed his face. "So am I. So am I. But not how you mean. I don't believe they did it. Tribeca was headed back to California when Grunt was gutted. So much for that theory."

"Apparently not."

"How do you know all this? You got no proof."

"I don't, you're right. Not for sure. But my intuition tells me..."

"I don't buy that wacko Montaukett Indian hocus pocus. Besides, the Appendage confessed. She's a nut bag I know, but Teddie might lock her up, and that's the end of it. Are you gonna tell me you wouldn't be happy about that? Chase is getting married for Christ sakes."

"I hear you. I also hear another voice telling me that isn't what happened."

"Don't listen to that voice. Simple."

Em smiled. "I won't tell another soul, Dragger, but you have to at least entertain the idea that..."

"Don't finish it, Em. I swear I'm on the edge here. I need a fucking drink."

Dragger put his jacket on and grabbed his smokes off the coffee table.

"Where are you going?"

"None of your business. To talk to Chase."

"I advise against it."

"Who asked you?" Dragger slammed the door and climbed into his truck.

Em reached for her cell and punched in Chase's number.

Chapter Fifty-Three

The whore boat would be docked for a few days at least. The nor'easter was picking up steam. Dragger knew where he could find the Admiral. He put off talking to Chase, for now. The conversation with Em had rattled him. He wanted to punch something. He pulled alongside the Admiral's truck at Liars. He held onto the door of his truck, the wind was blowing like a bastard. He put his head down and walked briskly up the wooden planks to the front door.

Sin was behind the bar. It was late afternoon and already the booze and bullshit were flying like a hungry flock of seagulls. Dragger took off his wet jacket and hung it on a hook on the back door. He sat down next to the Admiral. "Admiral."

"Dragger, my boy, bad one coming. What brings you out? Looking for Earl Grey perhaps? I haven't seen him today."

"No, I ain't looking for Ass. What's she doing here?" Dragger looked at the Appendage sitting on the other side of the Admiral.

"Bridget O'Malley and I were reminiscing about the old days in town…"

"Spare me. Sin, pour me a Jameson, neat."

"I will not. Sorry, Dragger, it ain't happening."

The Admiral put his arm around Dragger's shoulder. "Captain, may I have a word with you in private?"

"Not now, Admiral, I'm on a mission. Hey Sin, give me a break, just one short one."

"No way." She filled a glass with Coke and pushed

it towards him. "On the house."

"Thanks for nothing. Can't even get a fucking drink around here…"

The Admiral persisted. "Now, Dragger, let's sit down over by the window. Bridget, you'll excuse us, won't you?"

The Appendage nodded her head and played with the lime in her vodka and tonic.

Dragger reluctantly followed the Admiral to the small table in the back. He was in no mood for the old man's witticisms today. He also knew better than to push his luck with a bar full of dry docked Saltys. And he was too old for a fight. The body knew it even if the mind did not. "Howling out there, Captain," The Admiral said, watching the pounding rain.

"Get to the point, Admiral, I'm hanging by a thread."

"Understood. Understood. Has this dark mood of yours got anything to do with the boat?"

"Not exactly."

"Hmm…Bridget O'Malley?"

"What is this, twenty questions?"

The Admiral tapped his glass of club soda. "I have a suggestion."

"Alert the press. Go ahead, I'm all ears," Dragger downed his Coke.

Why he agreed to have a chat with The Appendage alone, he would wonder for a long time. Chalk it up to Jack Daniels brain damage. She was sitting in his truck when he went outside. The Admiral stood by the door waving his arms "Go with the grace of God, son," he shouted out before the wind blew the door to Liars shut. Right. I need all the luck I can get, Dragger thought.

"Hi, Dragger. Miserable weather, huh?" the Appendage said.

"Miserable ain't the word for it." Dragger hung a right on West Lake and headed for his place.

"All I got is coffee," he said when they got upstairs and took off their wet coats.

"Good, I like coffee," the Appendage said.

Dragger threw a few pieces of wood in the woodstove and lit a match. "It'll warm up in a minute."

"Fine. Nice place. Must get lonely though…"

"Listen, I brought you up here to discuss business. So don't get any fucking ideas."

"I wasn't insinuating anything, I just…"

"Whatever. You want coffee? It ain't fresh but it's warm."

"Yes, thanks. Call me Bridget, the Admiral does."

The bitch was a pro, Dragger thought. Played the nutcase, but knew full well what she was doing. Dragger wasn't falling into this quicksand. He wanted a drink, not a blowjob. Steady mate, this one is a man eater.

"Hot coffee as promised. Now let's get down to business."

The Appendage blew on her coffee. "You are eager. I like that…" she licked her red glossy lipstick.

"We ain't fucking, you got that? And I don't require any of the services you provide the Admiral with either."

The Appendage smiled. "So you heard about me…I could drive you crazy, Dragger."

"Been there, more than once. No thanks. Give it a rest and just listen."

"Is it because I'm not a Mermaid?"

"No. Now let's talk about Grunt."

Dragger was not prepared for tears. Women could turn them on like a faucet in his experience and it unnerved him. At least with guys, you knew what the score was at all times. Tempers flared, fists were thrown and it was over. Miller Time. Not with women. They had this secret weapon at their disposal. The fucking crying game. It made Dragger nervous. He handed the Appendage a paper towel.

"Thanks. I just miss Grunt so much. No one talks about him anymore."

"Really? So why'd you carve him up?"

More tears. Jesus H. Christ. Dragger lit a cigarette and poured more coffee. The Appendage touched his wrist. Dragger flinched and banged down the coffee pot.

"I told you to cut the shit. You don't listen, do you?"

Quivering lip. This one was too much. Still, it got under his skin in a way he wasn't proud of. You're a simple beast, he thought of himself.

"I didn't kill Grunt. I loved him." The Appendage was all wide eyed innocence and the words came out in a baby whisper. What was she, a ventriloquist?

"The Admiral told me you confessed. Or at least Bridget O'Malley did."

"It was a game. I like games, don't you? Do you have any nuts?"

Dragger choked on his coffee. "Why, are you going to pretend to be a squirrel?"

The Appendage laughed. "No, I'm trying to stay off sweets. Nut are full of protein."

"So is blood."

"That's not funny. I'm not a vampire, Dragger."

Oh boy, where this conversation could go was not pretty. Or safe. Time to bring it to a close and remain intact and get her the hell out of his house. While he still had his nuts. She was talking again. The baby voice was gone, replaced by a smoky sexy timbre with a hint of a lilt. Bridget O'Malley herself.

"We were lovers, Grunt and me. Wild nights we had. But he couldn't keep his hands off that Mermaid. That new one. I was jealous, I admit it. But I still loved him. I wouldn't hurt him. He never hurt me. But I knew he had a dark side. You could see it in his eyes. A blackness."

"Thanks for the revelation. So who did carve up the bastard?"

"You didn't like Grunt, did you? A fishing thing with you two, huh?"

"No, not at all. I don't like men who rape women."

The return of the tears. Here we go...

"How about your husband?"

"Hah. He couldn't find a cock in a hen house. Plus he's not that strong. Grunt would have crushed him." She smiled. The thought pleased her for some reason. "I have a little secret, Dragger." The baby whisper again. "Want to know what it is?"

"Only if it relates to Grunt's murder."

"Can I use the loo, first?"

"Sure, Bridget, help yourself. Second door on the left."

Dragger walked over to the window and watched the storm. Not a boat in sight. Everyone was tucked inside for the night. He remembered being offshore in a storm and wondering if he would make it back to see his daughter. Fate had other plans for him other than the briny depths. He wondered if he would have been better off if he wasn't so lucky. He hadn't heard her come back into the room but she was standing behind him. Hopefully without a blade to his back. He turned around. The Appendage/Bridget O'Malley was stark naked.

"You confess better when you have your clothes off, Bridget?"

"I do. It's a secret I'm telling you, remember?"

"Whatever. So spit it out." She didn't have a bad body. And she knew it. And she knew Dragger's weakness for women. "There's a condition…"

"Of course there is."

"I want you to call me 'Mermaid' while I please you, and then when we're both happy, I'll tell you who killed Grunt."

"Happy, as in ending?"

"You're very smart," Bridget O'Malley purred.

At the end of an otherwise miserable day, I knew two things. The Appendage could give a decent blowjob. My daughters were murderers.

234

Chapter Fifty-Four

It's a bald faced lie that a small town has no secrets. Everyone is so chummy chummy, the skeletons just come falling out of the closets on their own. Doesn't happen. Lake had kept her secret for more than forty years. Along with some key people being privy to it as well. No one was talking. Chase's mother least of all. The dead don't tell tales and Mrs. Hooker wasn't the journal keeping type. It was Maybelle Hooker who wrote about Chase's birth and left those letters in her attic. Her daughter had a comfortable enough life and that made it worth her while to stay quiet where Chase's gene pool was concerned. And she had Chase. The gift of a child to the childless is not something one takes for granted. Maybe she wasn't mother of the year, but she loved that girl and despite her penchant for bringing men home, the kid did okay, in spite of her.

A small town protects its own. That much was true. And it would remain true as far as her daughters were concerned, Lake would make sure of it. She was the calm voice of reason in this situation and that would serve her at the end of the day. A meeting with Tribeca and Chase would ease not only their minds, but her own. She would do what she had to do after that. It was up to her. She did not live this long and establish herself as an upright citizen, good mother, well-liked proprietor of a downtown shop, and member of the Montauk Morality Mission, for nothing. The last bit made her smile. Some morals lately, missy. Nobody's perfect.

The only cloud that ever hung over Lake, was living over her parent's old bait shop. She would never be free of Dragger Delray, until her dying day. Or his. Whichever came first. She remembered Maybelle Hooker's words the day Lake gave birth to the twins. "You'll tell Dragger nothing. You had one baby girl. That's all he ever has to know. The rest is between me, you, and God. You are doing my daughter a huge service, giving her a baby she could never have on her own. I'll sort out my own part in this when I meet my maker."

Until now, Maybelle had been right. Or had she? Dragger should have known. It would have prevented... no use thinking about it. What's done is done. The only thing that mattered now was saving her daughters from a life behind bars. She would make sure that never happened. Had she made another decision forty years ago, Chase would not have been on a whore boat in the first place. Lake had kept her promise to Chase's mother to see to her education, make sure she left Montauk and saw a bit of the world before settling down anywhere. Who thought it would be Dragger she had to protect her daughter from? This was all his fault. Or is it yours, Lake? She had to ask herself that question. After all Dragger didn't know Chase was his daughter, until recently. No, it was Lake's job to clean up this mess. She knew just where to start.

Chapter Fifty-Five

Lake lit a fire in the old fireplace and sipped her coffee. The wind was whipping up outside and it sang down the chimney. No one knew she was here and that she realized now was probably not in her favor. The Appendage was a nutter, everyone knew that. There was no telling what she might do when cornered. But she agreed to meet Lake at the old Tudor cottage on the bluffs out at Camp Hero. It belonged to a client of Lake's and he often let her use it when he was out of town. It was a great place to disappear for awhile. Lake loved to meditate on the bluff. Or as Dragger used to say "in the buff." One track minded man.

Anyway, seclusion was on their side, the summer people were long gone. But this was not a romantic rendezvous. Nor a friendly chit chat over tea. This was a stand-off and Lake was nervous. Maybe she should call Dragger? No, this was hers to do, alone. Maybe the Appendage changed her mind. Lake took her coffee and went over to the picture window, the last light of day turned the sky crimson. A sliver of moon hung as if painted for detail. Lake stared at the moon. Don't let this be a mistake, she thought. A flash of green silk crossed her line of vision. Show time.

She let the Appendage inside and watched as she unwrapped herself from two layers of green silk around her neck and rubbed her hands at the fire. "Getting wickedly cold out there for Fall. Going to be a cold winter, acorns are everywhere," she said, looking into the flames.

"Yep. The snowbirds will be flying the coop soon. Business is already slowing down."

"I'd love some coffee…"

Lake moved towards the kitchen. "Right. Sorry. How do you take it?"

"Cream, two sugars."

"I'll be right back," Lake said.

When she returned to the living room, The Appendage had made herself comfortable. She stretched her long legs to the fireplace's ledge and had removed her shoes. She had on two different colored socks. "Here you go…" Lake handed her the mug of coffee. "Thanks. So to what do I owe this pleasure? We aren't exactly bosom buddies, now are we?" The Appendage smiled. Her eyes glistened. Peridot, Lake thought. Green, the heart Chakra. Our relationship to others. Do we push away or draw in?

"Hello? Lake? What's the occasion? Is anyone else coming?"

"No. Like who?"

"Dunno. It's your party." The Appendage slurped her coffee noisily.

Lake tapped her cup. "Truth is, I have to ask you a favor."

"Really? Would that favor involve your daughters?"

Lake tucked her hair behind her ears. "You mean my daughter?"

"You want to make this a game?"

"Fine. Yes, my daughters. What do you know?"

"Enough. Everything." The Appendage set her coffee mug on the fireplace ledge and stood up, stretching like a cat. "Can I use your loo?"

Lake pointed towards the kitchen. "Back through there, take a right."

Lake stirred the fire and let her mind wander. How could she convince the Appendage to keep quiet about her girls? What was in it for her? Would a nice check do the trick? Lake could pay, no problem. But would that go on for years, until one day she decided to tell someone what she knew about Tribeca and Chase? Lake looked over at the couch. The Appendage's green scarf was thrown across the back of it. Or, I could strangle her, Lake thought, laughing to herself. As if. She couldn't even step on an ant.

"Let's go howl at the moon," the Appendage practically skipped into the room, startling Lake.

"Isn't that done on a full moon?" Lake looked into the peridot eyes again. Something had changed. The Appendage was almost giddy. He cheeks were flushed. Did she do a hit of LSD in the loo? She wasn't stoned, but she wasn't herself either.

"It's chilly outside, you said so yourself, remember?"

"Are ye afraid of a wee bit of wind, darlin'?" The Appendage swooped up her scarf and wrapped it twice around her neck. "To the bluff we go, Lake. Come on, don't be afraid. A quick howl and we'll be inside and warm again. Are you always the good girl?"

"Bridget?"

"Who else is here?"

"Fine, have it your way." Lake threw on her jacket and followed the Appendage outside.

Time and nor'easters had not been kind to

the bluffs of Montauk. Each year the land wore away from erosion and the bluffs shrank. You could stand dangerously close to the edge and it would just drop off, a long distance to the sea below. Lake watched as the Appendage danced around the front of the house as if in a trance. She grabbed Lake's hands and howled like a banshee. "Dance with me girl, swing me around. We're in this web together." Lake tried to pull free but the Appendage was strong and held tight. Faster, Lake, spin us faster..." She started to sing. *"Oh Bridget O'Malley, you left my heart shaken, with a hopeless desolation, I'd have you to know...and your beauty will haunt me wherever I go...* Sing it with me, Lake!" The peridots were on fire. Lake sang along with her as they held hands and spun around in a frenzied circle. "Keep looking at me," the Appendage demanded. "Keep your eyes on mine, we are one in our ritual. One in our love of men who have used us and thrown us away..." this last bit she said in a singsong lilt.

Lake caught a glimpse of the moon and looked down. They had danced to the edge of the bluff. The Appendage was facing her and Lake's back was towards the edge. She's going to run at me and I am going to die, Lake thought.

It was a split second in time. Lake fell over to the right, sprawling the two women on the ground. The Appendage was laughing hysterically. She unraveled her scarf, wrapped it around Lake's neck and got up and walked back towards the cottage. Lake caught her breath and got up to follow her. "That was crazy. What the hell were you thinking? You could have killed us both!"

The peridots stared at her. The Appendage started her song again. "*Oh Bridget O'Malley, you left my heart shaken...the big man is ashes and now he won't come to me, come to me...*I'll come to you, Gunther, my love, Bridget will come to you..."
The Appendage let go a keening wail that Lake would hear in nightmares for a long time, as she took off running towards the edge of the bluff.

Chapter Fifty-Six

Dragger made a mental note to buy Wilkinson a beer. The new Supervisor and the Town Board's bonehead move to try to sell the commercial fishing docks took the heat away from Grunt's unsolved murder case. The Saltys were up in arms and rightly so. The whole of Montauk was scratching their heads. What's next, they thought, a 711? Dragger was glad his old man wasn't around to see it. He used to tell Dragger, " With people, son, count on two things. Everybody has a shelf life. Most people have a price."

Dragger was as pissed off as the rest of the fishermen. You don't sell off people's livelihood to pay the town's bills, that was just wrong. If you strip Montauk of fishing, what do you have left? Eroding beaches and a lot of bars? There's no way the Town Board's plan could hold water, pardon the pun. But right now, Dragger was glad everyone had something else to occupy their minds, besides a dead whore boat captain.

There had to be another explanation for who gutted Grunt. Accepting that Chase and Tribeca were responsible was like believing the moon was made of green cheese. Madness. Total madness. Now the Appendage, that was another story. If they could get her to make a statement, somehow trick her into thinking she could remain on the whore boat if she did this one favor for the Admiral… it could work. Claim self- defense or temporary insanity, well in her case that was a stretch. Permanent insanity? That might work. At this point anything was worth a try.

Dragger felt his phone vibrate in his pocket. Lake's number appeared on the screen. Now what? He wasn't in the mood for her right now. She had this way of looking through him and if she smelled the Appendage, he might as well roast his own balls over an open fire. Not that he owed her any allegiance. He just didn't feel like listening to her, that's all. Truth was, he was still seething about her recent soul baring. Yet how could he tell her about Tribeca and Chase? She wouldn't be able to handle that. He was not handling it well himself. She would blame him. It was always his fault at the end of the day. His phone vibrated again. Lake. Relentless damn woman. Some things never change. He answered, knowing he would regret it later.

"Dragger, thank God, you're there. She's dead. She jumped right off the godforsaken bluff. I couldn't stop her. What are we going to do?"

We? "Wait. Slow down. Who's dead?"

"The Appendage. Bridget O'Malley, whoever she is. I'm telling you she dragged me to the edge and I thought we were both going to die. My life flashed before my eyes. She's crazy, Dragger. Well, I mean she was...I didn't know who to call."

Lucky me. "Hold on, hold on, where the hell are you?"

"Out at the old Tudor, by the Beard place. She's just laying down there, Dragger, all twisted and smashed on the rocks...Oh God, I never expected this to happen... why did I invite her here?"

Playing Sherlock fucking Holmes again, Lake?

How about solving the Case of the Twin Daughter Murderers? "You sure you didn't give her a shove?" "Fuck you."

Dragger smiled to himself. "I'll be right there."

Chapter Fifty-Seven

The East Hampton Star's headline on Thursday: **Love, Murder, Suicide**. "Myrna Sinclair, known as The Appendage, found dead on Camp Hero Beach, confessed to the murder of Gunther "Grunt" Schmidt, just minutes before her fatal jump off the bluff in front of the old Tudor, next to Peter Beard's place in Montauk. Apparently despondent over her lover's gruesome murder, which she and her estranged husband, Grady Sinclair carried out earlier this month; Mrs. Sinclair could not live with the guilt and took her own life. The oral confession, taped by Lake Delray and given to Chief of Police, Teddy Tooker, is considered evidence in the Gunther Schmidt murder. Mrs. Sinclair will serve no jail time as she has gone on to her final judgment. Mr. Sinclair, however, was arrested this morning and arraigned in East Hampton Town Court. He denied all involvement in the Gunther Schmidt killing. He was heard screaming: "I'm telling you those bitches done it..." as he was led to the jailhouse.

Dragger swallowed the rest of his coffee, wadded up the front page and threw it into the woodstove. He could live with Grady Sinclair going to jail more than he could stand the sight of his daughters in prison garb. But still it wasn't right. Grady's only mistake was marrying the Appendage. Misfortunate bastard. They would eventually let him go; they had no hard evidence against him. He didn't confess, she did. He wasn't the expert with a filet knife. And for that reprieve, Grady kept his mouth shut about Tribeca and Chase. Grunt was a closed chapter for all of them.

The whore boat sailed again for a good while. Admiral Flapjaws was on his game despite not having Bridget O'Malley to sing him to sleep any longer. Em saw to it a younger replacement took care of amusing the Admiral. The boat was prosperous and steady as far as the Mermaids. The Montauk Morality Mission was busy with the coming summer tourists. Where to put the parking overflow for the Smurf Lodge was their big concern. The blizzard of 2013, strangely named Nemo, hammered Montauk and with houses out at Culloden and the ocean hanging by a thread off the now eroded cliffs, FEMA had to get involved. No one had time to pay attention to a quiet boat that went out of the Harbor and came back in without any fanfare. What took place "in the middle of the ocean," remained out there. Those who indulged stayed quiet. Those who didn't did the same.

Aspen and Chase had their wedding. A tasteful affair, on a warm June night, starting with a ceremony at sunset on the beach. It was officiated by a Buddhist monk friend of Lake's, an Episcopalian minister uncle of Aspen's who flew in from Surry, and the Admiral Joey Flapjaw's himself, who still held a license to perform weddings. Dragger figured they were covered on all counts, but he gave them his own blessing nonetheless.

"Be happy. Don't piss each other off. Make love not war. And remember, Ass, she knows how to filet a fish…" The last bit he whispered.

Tribeca served as the matron of honor and both Lake and Dragger walked Chase down the aisle, or sand path, as it were. Chase had asked them to do it together. "So I can finally feel like I belong to this family," she told them. Em was a bridesmaid, as well as Sin and a few of the Mermaids. Chase wore white. The girls wore blue. A deep ocean blue. They carried pussy willows from Big Reed.

There was a reception to follow at Gurney's. Dragger footed the bill. He insisted. Lake knew it was his way of eliminating whatever demons he was struggling with concerning Chase. Lake was just happy they could all be in the same room and enjoy themselves without drawing blood. Keeping the anger going for another decade wasn't on Lake's agenda. What Dragger decides to do with it all, she thought, she had no control over. He was sober, he knew about Chase and didn't bite Lake's head off, he managed to keep their daughters out of jail, and now he was walking towards her…

"Dance?"

"Why not? But can I just say one thing first?"

"Don't spoil the moment, Lake. Give it a rest for once."

"You know what? Never mind. Let's just dance."

Dragger held his heart. "You trying to kill me? You're actually giving in?'

Lake laughed. "Don't get comfortable. It's temporary."

Aspen and Chase spent their honeymoon in Surry and took a trip to the Mediterranean for a month afterwards. Chase decided she liked his grandmother's cottage so much she wanted to stay in Surrey and raise little Aspens. Ass as usual was agreeable. The whore boat had served its purpose. Dragger was thinking about a shack down in the Keys. The Admiral was dreaming of Costa Rica and a Mermaid he took a fancy to was eager to join him. The old guy knew how to charm them. Em couldn't leave Montauk for good. Big Reed called her; her roots were too deep. But a vacation cottage in Aruba sounded good to her. Tribeca returned to Cali with her husband. She would make frequent visits to Surrey and be a good auntie to Chase's brood. Four little girls, ages like stepping stones, hair all blonde ringlets and eyes like green seaweed.

"We have our own little fleet of mermaids," she joked to Aspen one day. He winced, then smiled. "I prefer fairies or pixies, if it's all the same to you, love."

"Will we ever tell them what we all did once upon a time? I mean when they are older, of course."

"They wouldn't believe it was real, I'm sure. Would you?"

Epilogue

Sometimes you need people. In short spurts, mind you. That keeps it uncomplicated. I settled into a simple life for the rest of my days. Excitement is overrated anyway. Easy for you to say, old Salty. You ran a whore boat way past middle age. Did things most people only fantasize about. And earned a new title, Grandpa. That one wasn't easy to swallow, but it beat the dirt nap.

I looked out at the water. It wasn't Montauk Harbor but the Keys have been good to me. Hooking up with River Denero and having his boat at my disposal wasn't a bad gig. Heaven was still in the picture. River had cured her of her casino bombing habit. These days she ran a small café called "Heaven on a bun." River said she made the best chili he ever tasted. I thought it was glorified sloppy joes, but I kept that bit to myself. Love could make chopped meat taste like filet mignon. Thankfully, love was not on my horizon. Catching fish for dinner was all that was on my mind.

River brought me a cup of coffee. "Good to have you aboard, Dragger. It's been awhile."

"Yeah, good to see you too, man. Nice boat. This place agrees with you. By the way, did I ever thank you for taking Heaven off our hands and saving the whore boat?"

"More than once. Not a problem. I'm a happy man."

"I can see that. This is the life all right. But it ain't Montauk, you know?"

"You got that deep in the blood, Dragger. I can't

help you there, but I can do something else..."

"Thanks, man, but I ain't into threesomes."

River laughed. "I wasn't offering. But seriously, I got to thinking, I have Heaven and my friend Dragger is all alone..."

"Listen, I ran a ship of Mermaids, do you think this old bastard needs a broad this late in the game?"

"This wouldn't be any woman, Dragger."

"Don't even think it."

River Denero was always a decent guy. Generous. Loyal. But this last favor he did for me I could have died without.

"Dragger, I just figured I have my Heaven and you should have your..."

"Hell?"

We caught four nice size grouper that day on River's boat. I grilled them in butter, white wine, lemon and shallots. River opened the wine. I had a Coke. Heaven made the salad. There wasn't a bone in any piece of fish. They had been filleted expertly. No, my daughters weren't visiting. But thanks to River, their mother was in town, and as Maybelle Hooker would say: "They didn't lick it off the ground." Turns out Lake had another secret up her sleeve. I decided I'd heard enough the last time. It makes a guy nervous to know all the women in his life are handy with a knife. Grunt, you pissed off the wrong women, Sporty. And you said I didn't share.

27833413R00142

Made in the USA
San Bernardino, CA
18 December 2015